CW01468279

OTHER BOOKS BY ANNABELLA MICHAELS

Souls of Chicago Series:

Feeding the Soul, Book 1

Music of the Soul, Book 2

Protecting the Soul, Book 3

Renewing the Soul, Book 4

Constructing the Soul, Book 5

Uniting the Souls, Book 6

Ever-Greene, Book 7 (A holiday novella)

Hamilton's Heroes Series:

Found, Book 1

Jay,

Thank you so much
for your friendship.

Love,
Annabella
Michaels

THE
SWAP

ANNABELLA MICHAELS

The Swap
Copyright © 2018 Annabella Michaels

annabellamichaels.blogspot.com

This is a work of fiction. Names, characters, places and incidents either are the product of the author's imagination or are used fictitiously, and any resemblance to actual person, living or dead, business establishments, events or locales is entirely coincidental.

Cover art provided by Jay Aheer of Simply Defined Art—www.jayscoversbydesign.com

Editing provided by Allison Holzapfel

Proofreading provided by Judy Zweifel of Judy's Proofreading, www.judysproofreading.com

Interior Design and Formatting provided by Stacey Blake of Champagne Book Design, www.ChampagneBookDesign.com

All rights reserved. This book is licensed to the original publisher only.

This book contains sexually explicit material and is only intended for adult readers.

Copyright and Trademark Acknowledgments

The author acknowledges the copyright and trademarked status and trademark owners of the following trademarks and copyrights mentioned in this work of fiction:

Ghost: Paramount Pictures
Disneyland- The Walt Disney Company
Winnie-the-Pooh- A.A. Milne
The Cosmopolitan Magazine- Hearst Communications
Vogue Magazine- Conde Nast
THOR- Marvel Studios
Emmy Awards- Academy of Television Arts & Sciences
IN-N-OUT Burger- Harry & Esther Snyder
Robin Roberts- Good Morning America- ABC News Productions
Armani- Giorgio Armani
Forbes Magazine- Forbes Media, LLC.
Los Angeles Lakers- Buss Family Trusts
Los Angeles Police Department
Coke- The Coca-Cola Company

Possible trigger warnings: This book contains situations of physical violence which may be disturbing to some readers.

DEDICATION

This book is dedicated to all of you who encouraged and pushed me to finish this book. Your messages, calls, sprinting time and yes, sometimes even tough love were what got me through. You know who you are, and I am so blessed to have each and every one of you in my life. I love you.

THE
SWAP

ONE

Samuel

I stared down at my watch. Was the second hand moving faster than usual? It seemed like it was spinning out of control, dragging me closer and closer to the inevitable moment that I'd been dreading. A feeling of doom settled over me and my stomach clenched uncomfortably, threatening to expel its contents.

A hand reached out and covered my own. The fingers were narrow, their nails painted in a shimmery, pale pink polish. A delicate silver ring adorned the index finger and a thin bracelet encircled the slender wrist. Turning my hand over, I weaved my fingers through hers, giving her a gentle squeeze. Looking up, I was met with a pair of eyes, the same shape and shade of blue as my own. She smirked at me.

"You know, we have things like cell phones and computers that we can use to communicate these days. It's not like when you were my age and had to chisel a message into a stone or send a letter by carrier pigeon," Brooklyn teased. She bumped my shoulder and I heard her tinkling laugh as I rolled my eyes.

"I'm only thirty-seven years old. I didn't *actually* ride dinosaurs to school, you know," I joked back, pasting a smile on my face.

Brooklyn saw through my façade though and I watched as her smile faltered.

"It'll be okay, Daddy. We can call and text whenever we want," Brooklyn reminded me, quietly.

Her eyes filled with sympathy and a quiet understanding as she gave me a watery smile. I cleared my throat, trying to dislodge the knot that had formed there. I was the parent, it was my responsibility to comfort and support her.

I wrapped my arm around her and she tucked her head under my chin, the way she'd done since she was a little girl. I dipped down and kissed the top of her head. The familiar scent of her favorite strawberry shampoo filled my nostrils and I squeezed my eyes shut as I breathed in deep. I was going to miss this, miss *her* so much.

I opened my eyes and saw Gayle staring at the two of us. Her lips were pressed tightly together as she tried to rein in her emotions, but her eyes filled with tears as they met mine. I reached for her and pulled her into our hug. She rested her forehead against Brooklyn's back and I heard her choke back a sob.

We held each other quietly, lost in our own thoughts and memories. A few moments later, I checked my watch. "It's time, honey," I said quietly. I wanted to take the words back as soon as I said them, but I couldn't. We slowly untangled ourselves and stood. I froze when I saw the panicked look in Brooklyn's eyes. I could wallow in my own misery later, but right then, my daughter needed me. She needed me to be strong, to reassure her that she was doing the right thing and that she'd be okay.

I cupped her face in my hands and stared into her eyes. "You are my biggest joy and my greatest achievement. You've brought nothing but love and happiness into our lives and your mother and I are so proud of the young woman you've become. It's hard to let you go, but you have so much to offer the world and it would be selfish of us to keep you all to ourselves. This is *your* time, to explore, to learn and to figure out exactly who and what you want to be." I pressed my lips to her forehead and swallowed hard when she wrapped her arms around my waist and squeezed.

"But what about you and Mom?" she asked in a shaky voice.

"We'll be fine. Maybe we'll actually take up some new hobbies," Gayle spoke up. I gave her a grateful look and she winked at me. We'd always made a good team when it came to parenting and this time was no different.

Brooklyn chuckled as she let go of me and turned to her mother. "You mean like salsa dancing and couples pottery classes?" she teased, then a look of horror crossed her face. "Oh God! Please, promise me you won't be one of those gross couples that tries to act out that scene from Ghost," she begged, her nose wrinkling in disgust.

"Get over here and give me a hug, you twerp." Gayle laughed, and I felt a genuine smile spread across my face as I watched them embrace.

Another announcement rang out. "You'd better get going, sweetheart. You don't want to be rushed trying to find your seat," I said gently.

Brooklyn pulled back and looked at us. "I love you both so much. Thank you for everything you've done." Fresh tears swam in her eyes and she kissed her mother's cheek and then threw her arms around my neck. "I love you, Daddy," she whispered in my ear and I hugged her tightly, committing to memory the feel of her in my arms.

"I love you too, you'll always be my best girl," I promised. We hugged for a few more seconds and then I cleared my throat and pulled back, giving her a smile.

Memories assaulted me. The day Gayle and I had brought her home from the hospital, both of us scared out of our minds because we were barely more than children ourselves. Her first steps, first Christmas, first sleepover. The dance recitals and softball games, the science fairs and school plays. The weeks when we raced home to check the mail, eager to see if Brooklyn had been accepted to the school of her choice, and then the day it finally came and the three of us danced in the kitchen.

I was so damn proud of her and not at all surprised that she'd reached her goals and earned a full-ride scholarship to one of the best colleges in the country. She'd always been a very determined child, and a hard worker. However, reality had slowly started to sink in for me and Gayle that she was actually going to be moving out of our home and attending a college nearly three thousand miles away.

Gayle and I had committed that summer to spending as much time with our daughter as possible. We'd enjoyed camping, white water rafting, and even carved out time to visit Disneyland. We'd spent countless nights watching movies together and sitting around talking until the wee hours of the morning. We'd soaked up as much time together as we could, but before we knew it, the weather had started to cool, and autumn had arrived.

The time had come that every parent dreaded. It was time to let go. Brooklyn picked up her carry-on bag and I watched as she drew in a deep breath and pulled her shoulders back. I knew how scared she was, but I could also see the strength and determination in her posture. A burst of pride filled me. My girl was going to do just fine on her own.

I reached for Gayle and she sidled up to me, wrapping an arm around my waist as we watched our daughter walk to the security gate. My breath caught as Brooklyn turned back to us and we waved to her robotically. She walked backward as she blew a final kiss our way and then she disappeared around the corner. We stood frozen, as if we almost expected her to come running back through the gate, shouting "Just kidding!" The minutes dragged on, each of us unwilling or unable to move until someone bumped into me, pulling me out of my daze.

"We should go," I murmured.

Gayle began to cry, and I wrapped my arms around her, pulling her tightly against my chest. Her arms slid around me, but I didn't trust myself to speak so I simply rocked her back and forth until her cries settled into soft hiccups.

I held her hand as we moved numbly through the airport. It suddenly seemed too bright and too loud as people raced past us to get to their planes on time. It was too painful to watch as people rushed forward in joy as they were reunited with loved ones. I felt raw and exposed, and I found myself walking faster and faster, pulling Gayle along behind me.

Finally, we made it back to our car and I was surprised to hear Gayle let out a relieved sigh as we climbed inside. I glanced over and found her staring out the window, her face pale and her cheeks streaked with dried tears.

"She'll be alright, won't she?" Gayle asked. Her voice was small and cracked on the last word.

The backs of my eyes itched as tears threatened once again, but I forced them back. I cleared my throat. "She's all the best parts of the two of us. She'll be more than alright. She's going to shine," I assured her.

Gayle turned to face me, and she nodded her agreement, even as fresh tears splashed over her cheeks. I reached into the glove compartment and handed her a small container of tissues. She thanked me, and I waited as she wiped her tears and blew her nose.

"Are you hungry? We could stop somewhere and get something to eat if you'd like," I offered. My own stomach roiled at the thought of food, but it would make me feel a little less helpless if I could focus my attention on taking care of her. Gayle shook her head though and let out a heavy sigh.

"Can we just go home, please? I'm tired," she said. I could see the weariness in her expression and I tucked her hair behind her ear.

"Of course. Whatever you want," I said gently.

I started the car and winced as the small space was filled with the grinding beat of one of Brooklyn's favorite songs. I stabbed the buttons of the radio with my fingers until it turned off and we were once again bathed in silence.

The drive home was quiet without our daughter's constant chatter coming from the back seat. I pulled into our driveway and parked before shutting off the engine. I stared out the window at the house that had always been so full of energy and life. Now, it loomed ahead of us, suddenly seeming too big for just the two of us.

Neither of us spoke as we climbed from the car and made our way inside. I flipped the light on and tossed my keys into the bowl on the table near the door while Gayle hung her jacket on the coat rack.

"Do you want a cup of tea or something to snack on?" I asked.

"No, thank you. It's been a long day. I think I'm just going to go to bed," she answered quietly.

"Okay. I'll be up in a little while," I told her, but she was already moving away and toward the stairs.

A sinking feeling started in the pit of my stomach and spread throughout my body. It wasn't a completely unfamiliar feeling. Gayle and I had been living as nothing more than friends for over a year, but we'd worked hard to hide it from our daughter. With Brooklyn off discovering a life of her own, the distance between my wife and me was glaringly obvious and threatened to choke me.

I went to the kitchen and grabbed a glass, filling it with water and drinking it down as I leaned against the counter. My eyes landed on a smiling photo of Brooklyn and my chest began to ache. Pulling the picture from its magnet, I studied the wide smile on my daughter's face. I wanted her to stay that way always; happy and carefree. I just wished it didn't have to hurt so bad to let her go.

With a sigh, I returned the picture and then walked through the house, turning off lights and locking the front door. I felt older than my thirty-seven years as I climbed the steps. When I reached the top of the stairs, I looked in the direction of our bedroom. The lights were off, and it was quiet. I assumed that Gayle was already asleep.

I knew that I could go to Gayle and seek comfort in her arms and that she would be there for me. She was still, after all, my best friend. But I also knew that it would feel empty, missing the components that made what would occur truly intimate. It was that emptiness that had eventually led us to being just friends.

I turned instead and headed into Brooklyn's room. Moonlight streamed through the curtains, lighting the room enough that I was able to make out the poster of a popular boy band hanging on the wall and the stack of books on her bedside table. A lump formed in my throat as I looked at her desk, which used to hold her laptop and a slew of notebooks, but which now stood empty.

Then my eyes lowered to the bed and my eyes welled with tears when I saw she'd left her favorite Winnie-the-Pooh doll. There'd been a time when he'd accompanied us on every car trip, and I'd often have to turn back home to the sound of her sobs because she'd forgotten him. The fact that she'd left him behind proved that she'd moved on, outgrowing him as she transitioned into adulthood.

That thought hit me like a ton of bricks and I sank onto the bed. I grabbed the bear and buried my face into his plush form as my tears finally broke free, no longer needing to hide them from anyone. I cried for the little girl I missed and the marriage that was no longer true. I had no idea what would become of our little family, and at the moment, I was too tired to try and figure it all out.

At some point, I must've drifted off, because it was several hours later when my phone chirped beside me. I grabbed it and swiped the screen quickly to open the text message.

We just landed, and I wanted you to know I arrived safely. The flight was a long one and gave me a lot of time to think. You said that this was my time to explore and figure out who I want to be, but the same could be said for you guys. You and Mom deserve to have fun now that you don't have to plan your schedules around my activities. You've sacrificed everything for me and you're the best parents any girl could ask for, but it's time that we all figure out who we're supposed to be from here on out. I don't want you to be sad while I'm gone. Find what makes you happy, Daddy. I love you more than chocolate cake.

I smiled as I read her words and then I read them again. She was right. I needed to quit feeling sorry for myself and figure out what would make me happy. The problem was, I had no idea what that was.

TWO

Oliver

My back ached and every muscle in my body screamed its displeasure. I clenched my jaw, breathing deeply through my nostrils as I struggled to hold still.

"You look constipated," Korey said from across the room. He sounded rather pleased with himself. Sometimes, I wondered if he didn't enjoy my discomfort a little too much.

"Sorry," I muttered. I released the breath I'd been holding and tried to relax my face into a more serene expression.

"Ignore him. You're doing great," Ben whispered. He gave me a kind smile as he continued to move around me, dipping his body and turning the camera to get the right angle.

I looked at Korey out of the corner of my eye and saw him frown. He'd obviously heard what Ben said and didn't like it. There was definitely no love lost between the two men, but Korey knew better than to cross Ben. Ben had threatened to kick him out of his studio on more than one occasion and I had no doubt that he'd follow through on those threats if Korey pushed him.

Ben was the most sought-after photographer in the business and my favorite to work with. He'd worked with some of the top names in modeling and his photos could be seen in every fashion magazine, from Cosmo to Vogue. I was honored that he was willing to work with me, especially given how he and Korey butted heads. But Ben was always nice to me and made the long hours pass more quickly by telling me stories of the places he'd traveled to and the people he'd worked with.

However, that day, I'd nearly reached my breaking point and even Ben's tales weren't distracting me from the pain I was in. We'd been at it for over six hours and my ass had long since gone numb from sitting on the unforgiving metal stool. My neck felt like it had a permanent kink in it and I could feel my composure starting to crumble. Surely, in the three thousand photos Ben had taken, there would be at least one that would be worth turning in to the magazine.

"Are we almost done?" I whispered through barely parted lips.

"Almost. I just want to get a few more now that the sun has finally decided to make its appearance. It's streaming through the windows and the way it's landing on your face…" He trailed off, his voice sounding reverent. I knew it was more about the lighting he was seeing filtered through his lens that was making him sound that way than my actual face. Ben was my friend. He liked me, but he was also very professional, and as far as I knew, very straight.

I held still as he took several more pictures. "You can relax now. I'm finished." I let out the breath I'd been holding and stood on shaky legs, my body screaming in protest of the abuse I'd put it through.

"I'll get started on the proofs right away and then send them over to the magazine. They'll let us know if they aren't satisfied with what we've provided, but I doubt that'll be the case. The camera loves you." He walked across the room to where his camera bag lay and began putting away the expensive equipment.

I tilted my head from side to side, trying to work the stiffness out of my neck then jumped as a pair of warm hands landed on my shoulders. I hadn't even heard Korey walking up behind me, but I let out a moan as his fingers started kneading my aching muscles.

"You've had a long day. I think you deserve a surprise," he whispered.

I looked over my shoulder, arching my brow at him. "What are you up to?"

"If I told you, then it wouldn't be a surprise now, would it?" Korey teased, wagging his eyebrows at me.

I turned back around at the sound of a throat clearing and flushed with embarrassment when I saw Ben standing in front of us. For a moment, I'd forgotten he was in the room. His eyes narrowed as he stared at the man behind me. I felt Korey tense up and his fingers dug into my shoulders, almost to the point of pain.

"Thank you so much for everything," I told Ben sincerely, trying to defuse the tension between the two men. I'd never understood why they disliked each other so much. Ben's eyes darted over to mine and the hard edge that had been there before disappeared as he smiled at me.

"As always, it was a pleasure working with you. I look forward to seeing you again." With that, he turned and left, but his emphasis on the word *you* had made it quite clear that he wasn't including Korey in his sentiments.

"Pompous asshole," Korey gritted out. "He obviously doesn't know who he's talking to. I should have him fired!"

I struggled not to roll my eyes, knowing it probably wasn't the best time to point out that Ben was an independent contractor and magazines hired him for individual projects because he was the best. He was his own boss and therefore couldn't be fired.

I turned to face him. "So, what's my surprise?" I asked, eager to change the subject.

Korey stepped away from me with a shake of his head. "You'll have to wait and see," he said, giving me a mischievous grin. I relaxed a bit with the return of his playful mood and smiled at him.

I quickly changed back into my own clothes, throwing everything into my bag and zipping it up. Korey was waiting for me at the front door and without a word, he reached for the heavy duffle bag I had on my shoulder. I could've carried it, but I let him take it instead, knowing he wouldn't listen even if I argued. He enjoyed taking care of me, claiming it was all part of his job as my agent. I disagreed, but it was easier to just let him have his way.

Korey and I had met three years earlier. I'd moved to Los Angeles just a year before and was still suffering a bit of culture shock. I'd grown up in a small town in Alabama, where being different was frowned upon. I never admitted to anyone back home that I was gay, especially not my father or mother. Although, I was pretty sure they suspected.

The older I got and tried to dress or style my hair the way I wanted, the more restrictions they put on me. They were never abusive, but they were controlling to the point of suffocation. I knew they acted that way because they were afraid. Afraid that one day I'd speak out about my "sinful thoughts" and the town's preacher would have to explain to his congregation that his only child was gay.

Not long after graduating high school, I moved to L.A. in hopes of finding a job somewhere in the fashion industry. I'd never expected to see so many other people like me. It was liberating, to say the least, and I immediately felt like I'd found my tribe, even though I hadn't actually met anyone yet.

I put my resume in every store, from the biggest names in the industry to tiny, corner boutiques. It didn't matter to me what job I got as long as I was able to work in fashion. After several weeks with no response and my savings dwindling, I was forced to get a job serving drinks in a swanky nightclub.

It was there that I met Korey. He'd come into the club with a group of friends, each of them more beautiful than the next, but somehow, I caught his eye. Despite having his friends there, Korey seemed more interested in getting to know me. He talked with me every time I came back to refill their drinks, and I responded, even though I was nervous as hell. I'd never met anyone quite as suave and sophisticated as him.

I admit to being naïve back then. Everything about the city was like an awakening for me, and Korey Duncan was no exception. He was still hanging around by the time my shift ended and asked if I wanted to go get something to eat. He took me to an all-night diner and we spent the rest of the night together, talking and getting to know each other.

He told me that he was a modeling agent and then proceeded to entertain me with stories about his travels and the models he'd worked with. I'd nervously admitted that I wanted to work in fashion. I'd never spoken my dreams out loud to another soul, but Korey didn't laugh at me. Instead, he'd taken a step back, tilting his head as he scrutinized me. His eyes swept over me, analyzing every inch as he shook his head from side to side. Just as I started to feel self-conscious, he explained that I was wasting my time trying to get a job as a personal shopper or window dresser. He told me that with my bone structure and willowy shape, he thought I had what it took to become a model. Once again, my world was opened up to new and wondrous possibilities.

From that point on, Korey helped me with everything. He had me groomed and polished and bought me a whole new wardrobe. I argued that I didn't feel right, letting him spend so much money on me; but he insisted, saying that if I wanted to be a supermodel then I needed to look like a supermodel.

He took me to several parties and nightclubs and introduced me to some very important people, including magazine editors and fashion designers. He used those opportunities to brag about me and I'd stare at him in awe. He worked with gorgeous people every day. The fact that he saw beauty in me was beyond flattering, if not a bit surprising. In my mind, I was still the same old Oliver from

Nowheresville, Alabama.

I was thrilled when I landed my first modeling job just a few weeks later. A designer from one of the parties had apparently liked my look and asked me to be in a fashion show for her new fall collection. I gained a lot of attention with my first gig and before long, offers started pouring in. Korey was obviously very good at his job. He was six years older than me and had been in the business longer. He had the knowledge and the connections to make things happen. It felt good to know that he cared about me enough to want to help.

Korey could tell how nervous I was, and he insisted on going with me to my various fashion shows and photo shoots. I felt bad that I was taking up all his time when I knew he had other clients he should be paying attention to. He brushed off my concerns though, telling me that his assistants could help the other clients and that getting my career up and running was his priority. The look in his eyes told me that he wasn't going to budge so I let it go. Still, I felt guilty and hoped I wasn't hurting his business in any way.

I worked hard and paid attention, trying to learn not only my job, but all the other aspects of the industry, from lighting during photo shoots to how the designers came up with their inspiration. Most of the people I worked with seemed to appreciate my interest in their work and no one ever seemed bothered by my endless questions. However, Korey warned me not to stick my nose too far into other people's business. He told me that everyone had a part to play and mine was to look pretty. I'd bristled at his words and he'd rushed to explain that he'd simply meant that if I looked good in their magazines or wearing their clothing, then more people would want to buy them. Therefore, I was helping not only my career, but theirs as well.

I could see his point, but it still didn't stop me from asking questions. I'd spent too many years keeping quiet about the things I loved so that I wouldn't upset my parents. Now that I was out on my own, I wanted to learn everything I possibly could about the fashion world.

Korey scowled as he pulled his car in front of my apartment. He didn't bother to shut off the engine and I didn't bother to ask him to come inside. "You can afford better," he started, but I held my hand up, cutting him off before he could say more. We'd had the same argument more times than I could count, and I was too tired to get into it with him again.

He didn't understand why I chose to stay in the same apartment that I'd first rented when I moved to L.A. instead of living in some high-rise overlooking the city. I'd tried to explain that for me, my little home represented my freedom. It was the first place I'd ever lived in where I was able to do or say or think anything I wanted, and no one would judge me. Korey just laughed and told me that I could have the same thing in a luxury condo.

Logically, I knew he was right. I no longer lived under my parents' strict thumb and wherever I chose to live, no one would ever make me hide who I was again. Still, the tiny brick apartment with the leaky faucets and the peeling paint was home to me. It held an important place in my heart and when I eventually decided to move on from it, it would be *my* decision and no one else's.

"Let's not start that tonight, okay?" I pleaded.

"Fine. You go get ready. I have a few errands to run but I'll be back to pick you up in a half hour."

"You sure we can't just order Chinese and watch a movie? I'm really beat," I asked hopefully.

"No way. You're too young to be huddled up in your house like an old lady," he teased. "Go have a shower. Maybe that'll wake you up."

"Fine, but if I'm going to go back out, I at least deserve to know where we're going."

Korey gave me a sly smile. "I made reservations for that French restaurant you've been wanting to try."

"Bel Amour?" My eyes widened in surprise. "How the hell did you get a reservation? I heard they're booked up solid for the next two years."

"You'd be surprised what I can make happen," he responded.

I threw my arms around his neck. "Thank you so much. You're the best," I gushed.

Korey laughed as he hugged me back. "Don't ever forget it. Now, go in there and get cleaned up before we miss our reservation time." I jumped out of the car, grabbed my duffle bag and, with a quick wave over my shoulder, ran up the sidewalk. Korey pulled away from the curb as I let myself inside.

I took a long hot shower, letting the water soothe the stiff muscles brought on by holding one pose for so long. My mind wandered, and I drifted away to my favorite daydream. It had started a few months before and was the same one every time. In my fantasy, I was held in the arms of my lover, the two of us spending a lazy day in bed together. We talked and made love and I fed him as we stared into each other's eyes. In my dream, I felt more connected to him than any other person on the planet.

I shut off the water with a sigh as the dream drifted away and reached for a towel. I dried myself and then wiped the steam from the mirror, noting the sadness in my reflection. I wondered if it would always be only a dream for me. Something I longed for but that was destined to remain just out of my reach. Was there even such a man out there who wanted the same things I did?

THREE

Samuel

"**B**urning the midnight oil again, I see," a voice said from the doorway. I looked up from my paperwork and saw Paul leaning against the doorway with his arms crossed.

Paul was my general manager and close friend. He'd been with me from the very start, working alongside me to make our agency one of the leading names in advertising. I wouldn't have gotten nearly as far without his expertise, or his friendship for that matter.

"Someone around here has to do it," I grumbled.

Paul's eyes narrowed, and he shut the door. Walking into my office, he sank down in the chair across from me. I stared at him warily. The frown he wore looked out of place on his usually smiling face and I knew he must have something important he needed to discuss.

"What's going on with you lately?" he asked, concern marring his features.

"What do you mean?" I could hear the defensive edge in my voice and I was sure that he'd picked up on it too because his jaw tightened.

"I mean, you've been working a ridiculous number of hours,

you're barking orders around here like a drill sergeant and you're putting everyone on edge," he stated firmly. "You act like you're trying to save a sinking ship, but the business is thriving. We have more clients than ever before, and we just landed another huge account. So, I'm going to ask again. What's going on with you?"

I pulled my reading glasses off and tossed them on top of my desk. I sighed wearily as I rubbed my eyes. I thought I'd been doing a good job of hiding my misery, but apparently, I was just making everyone else miserable along with me.

"I'm sorry. I didn't realize I was being an overbearing ass. I'll apologize to everyone in the morning," I assured him.

"You don't need to apologize. No one's angry, we're worried. We all care about you, Sam, and we know this isn't like you," he explained, his tone gentling.

My shoulders slumped. "I'm sorry. I guess I've just been in a slump since Brooklyn left for school. It's weird not having her at home, you know?"

I looked at my friend who gave me a sympathetic smile. Paul was married with three boys all under the age of ten, so he couldn't possibly know what it was like to feel like your life had lost some of its meaning, like you were suddenly set adrift after years of careful planning and whirlwind activity. He was still living a life filled with chaos and noise and trying to keep everyone on schedule. A pang of jealousy, sharp and swift, rushed through me. I pushed it aside, not wanting to feel that way toward my friend and knowing he didn't deserve it.

"I know you miss her a great deal; she's an amazing young woman. This is a great opportunity for you though. You can do all the things you weren't able to do before. You and Gayle can travel some, enjoy visiting places you've only dreamed of seeing before. Maybe take up golf or tennis," he suggested.

I knew he was only trying to be helpful, so I pasted a smile on my face. "You're right. I'm sure there's plenty I can do that will keep me busy and active. Can't let myself get fat and lazy," I joked. It sounded forced to me, but Paul must've bought it because he smiled, rapping his knuckles on the top of my desk.

"Now you're talking. Although, you don't have anything to worry about. You're in better shape than anyone else our age." He rolled his eyes as if annoyed by my physical appearance and when I laughed that time, it was more genuine.

"Okay, buddy. I'm going to get out of here. You should do the same. It's Friday night, take your lady out on a date," he suggested.

He stood, but he didn't make a move toward the door and I knew he was waiting to see if I'd follow his instructions. Paul had always been a worrier, but I couldn't fault him for it. It was that constant care that made him such an excellent friend. Silently, I gathered my things and followed him out the door.

It had gotten later than I'd realized, and I was surprised to see that it was dark outside. I was suddenly very grateful. Paul should've already been home, enjoying the weekend with his family, but instead he had stayed to check on me.

"I appreciate you talking to me. You're a really good friend," I said, slowing my steps as we neared his car.

Paul stopped and turned to me. "So are you. The very best. I know this hasn't been easy on you and I just want to know that you're alright."

We shared a quick one-armed hug and then I told him to go home and enjoy his family. He smiled at me and waved as he backed his car out of the lot. I climbed into my own car, but I didn't start the engine. Instead, I sat there, contemplating Paul's words.

The distance between me and Gayle had grown exponentially in the time since Brooklyn left. Where before, we still laughed and talked, now we easily went several days without saying a word to each other. I wasn't sure where we'd lost each other along the way, but I missed her. No matter what, she was the mother of my child and my best friend. Maybe Paul was right, and we just needed to spend more time together.

With that thought in mind, I started the car and began driving home. Along the way, I tried calling Gayle to see if she'd like to go out to dinner with me, but the call went straight to voicemail. I drove the rest of the way home, lost in my own thoughts as I tried to come up with a way to reconnect with my wife.

The house was dark when I got home, and Gayle's car wasn't in the garage. I tossed my keys on the table and made my way through the house, turning on lights as I went. The sound of a car pulling up the driveway caught my attention and I felt a bundle of nerves in the pit of my stomach. Things between Gayle and me had always been fun and easy, but now they were awkward and stiff. I hated the tension that had begun to surround the two of us whenever we were in the same room.

The door opened, and her eyes widened in surprise when she saw me standing there. For a moment, we just stared at each other. She looked tired. I'd heard her tossing and turning throughout the night, and knew she'd been getting as little sleep as I had. As strange as it may be, I found an odd sense of comfort in that, as if I weren't totally alone in my feelings.

I glanced down at the box she held in her hands then gave her a questioning look. She set it down on the table and then turned to me with a tentative smile. I couldn't stand the awkwardness anymore. This was Gayle. I knew her better than anyone else and she knew me. It was ridiculous that we were tiptoeing around each other.

"We need to talk," we both said at the same time. We stared at each other and then we started to laugh. It was nice, and it eased the tension immediately.

"I brought home a pizza. I thought maybe we could get in our jammies and just talk. Remember how we used to do that? Sometimes we'd stay up all night talking," she said wistfully.

"I remember," I answered. "Why don't you go on up and get

changed and I'll open a bottle of wine, so it can breathe."

I watched her walk away and then turned to the kitchen with a smile. This was exactly what we needed, the chance to clear the air and truly talk to one another. I had no idea what would come of it or where we'd end up, but it was a start.

I opened a bottle of red wine and then went upstairs to take a quick shower. By the time I got out, Gayle was already downstairs, so I pulled on a pair of sleep pants and a soft, cotton t-shirt and went back down to join her. Plates and napkins sat on the coffee table next to the pizza box and she walked in carrying the wine and two glasses. She smiled as she set them down and we both settled onto the couch.

"This was a good idea," I told her as we each grabbed a slice of pizza. We made small talk as we ate, mostly about Brooklyn and how she sounded the last time she'd called home. We'd been relieved to hear that she was settling in just fine at school. She enjoyed her classes and had made several new friends, including her roommate.

When she'd finished eating, Gayle set her plate aside and turned to face me. She leaned her back against the arm of the couch and folded her legs up under her. She'd always been a beautiful woman and even though we'd grown older, her beauty still remained. She shivered, and I pulled the blanket off the back of the couch, spreading it over both our legs. She thanked me, and then stared down into her wine glass, as if she wasn't sure where to start.

"We used to be able to say anything to each other. I know things have been strained since Brooklyn left, but you can still talk to me," I reminded her.

She gave me a grateful smile. "I've missed this. Missed talking with you. You've always been my best friend, but lately I've felt so distant from you. I hate it."

"I've felt it too and it makes me sad. We've always been a team. We learned pretty quickly when we became parents that we worked best when we worked together," I said.

"Do you ever wonder if that's all it was though?" She spoke so quietly that if I hadn't been facing her, I might have missed it.

"If that's all *what* was?" I held my breath, wondering if she was finally going to give voice to what I knew we'd both been feeling.

"If maybe we were just so scared, we had no choice but to cling to each other?" Her eyes flicked to mine and I saw a mixture of pain and fear. I reached out and took her hand in mine.

"I think we did what we had to do, and we made the absolute best of a very difficult situation. We both rose to the challenge and we raised an incredible child together," I answered honestly.

Gayle and I had met at a party our first year of college. We were both from small towns, raised by families with old-fashioned values and we were free for the first time in our lives. We started talking and I thought she was one of the brightest, funniest girls I'd ever met. We had a lot to drink that night, too much in fact, and we wound up having sex. A few months later, we found out that Gayle was pregnant.

We were both terrified, but I promised Gayle that I'd take care of her and the baby, that she wouldn't have to raise our child alone. We eloped the next day, shocking our parents who were furious. In a move that left us reeling, they told us we were on our own and swiftly cut all ties with us. They had since come around and were very involved in Brooklyn's life, but at the time, we were very much all alone and it had left wounds in each of us that would never fully heal.

Everything seemed to happen in fast-forward after that. We found a little apartment to rent and both got jobs. Gayle took a break from college and got a job waiting tables until she got further along in the pregnancy and could no longer be on her feet all day. I took out loans and attended evening classes at the local community college while spending my days working in a factory.

When Gayle was forced to quit working, I took on a second

job, but stayed in school. It was important to both of us that we be able to provide the best life we could for our child, and we knew having an education would help with that.

It was the most difficult time of our lives. We were scared to death, barely more than kids ourselves, and we were about to become parents. The stress of it all might have torn some couples apart, but it only served to strengthen the bond between us. Our friendship grew into a deep respect for each other and eventually turned into love. There was definitely love, but were we ever *in love* with each other?

"Do you think you would've married me if the decision hadn't been made for us by our careless choices?" Gayle asked. She stared at me with so much intensity, willing me to tell her the truth. I swallowed hard around the lump in my throat. I never wanted to hurt her. She tilted her head and smiled softly.

"I can see the answer just by looking at you. You've always had such expressive eyes. I've always known just what you were thinking and feeling in any situation by looking into your eyes." She squeezed my hand. "Would it help if I told you my answer would be the same as yours?" My breath whooshed out of me and I felt my shoulders slump.

"It would?" I asked weakly.

Gayle nodded. "Don't get me wrong. Brooklyn is the best thing that ever happened to me and I'll never regret having her, but by getting pregnant at such a young age, I never got to explore all the things I'd always wanted to do with my own life. I'm sure you had to have felt the same way."

"Of course. I wouldn't trade our daughter for the world. She's my heart, but there were things I would've done differently if she hadn't come along," I admitted.

"See, you said it right there. *She's* your heart, not me. The decisions you made were because of your love for her, not a burning need to be with me," Gayle pointed out.

"I do love you though." My words had a defensive edge and she held her hand up to stop me.

"I know you love me. I've never doubted that, and I love you too, but I think we can both admit that neither of us is in love with the other." She arched an eyebrow at me, daring me to deny her words.

I wanted to deny them. I wanted to tell her that she had it all wrong and that I was in love with her and could make her fall in love with me too. It would be so much easier and safer if we both just went back to pretending and lived out our lives in comfortable peace. I was nearly forty years old and the prospect of having to start over, of being single and trying to date again, filled me with an anxious dread.

But I couldn't bring myself to say those things. Gayle and I may not have been in love, but we did care for each other and we had built a solid relationship that was based on honesty. We'd done the right thing all those years ago and we had an incredible daughter to show for it, but things had changed when Brooklyn left for college.

We would always be her parents, but our everyday responsibilities toward her were no longer there. The time before us was ours again and we could do with it as we chose. Something sparked inside of me with that thought and my anxiety was replaced with anticipation over the possibilities.

"Yes, you're right," I answered carefully. She smiled at me then and I could see the relief in her eyes and a glimmer of something else and I wondered if she was feeling the same excitement I was.

"So, what happens now? Do we separate? File for divorce?" I asked. I felt an ache in my chest, but not the kind of pain I always thought I'd feel if the two of us ever split up. Perhaps it was because we both were in agreement about things. No one was getting their heart broken like what happened with so many other breakups.

"Let's take it slowly and play it by ear," Gayle suggested. "I think we should take the time to figure things out for ourselves before we say anything to Brooklyn."

"I think that's best. She's settling in well at school and I don't want to mess that up for her," I agreed.

"I don't know about you, but I only went on two dates in high school and then I met you. The idea of going out on a date is a little overwhelming," she admitted.

I puffed out my cheeks and released a breath slowly. "Yeah, it makes me a bit nauseous to think about being in the dating pool. I definitely don't want to do one of those dating sites. I refuse."

Gayle laughed at the expression on my face. "Well, I have an idea. Something that could be fun, and we can go together, kind of like a buddy system of sorts." She bit her lip as she stared at me.

"What is it?" I asked, immediately intrigued by the gleam in her eyes.

"Have you ever heard of a swap party?"

FOUR

Oliver

Sweat trickled down my back, soaking my shirt and causing the material to stick to my skin. Still, I kept going, my feet pounding the pavement in a steady rhythm. I'd been sprung like a tightly wound coil for the past week, but with each step, I felt the tension easing from my body.

Running had always had that effect on me. It was the only way I could pull myself out of a funk when I got too lost inside my own head. I'd been battling my own thoughts for over a week, but there'd been no chance to go running. Korey had scheduled multiple jobs for me that week, each of which took many hours to shoot. By the time we were finished each day, I could barely climb the steps to my apartment, much less work up the energy to go for a run.

A lot of people saw modeling as a fun and glamorous job, and for the most part, it was. I loved getting to wear the latest creations from world-renowned designers and I always had fun when I got to work with other models. But there were also a lot of times when it was just me and the photographer, the clicking of a camera the only sound in the room. Not all photographers were as fun or as easy to work with as Ben.

I'd learned early on that the only way to make it through those days was to let my mind wander. I'd drift away to the different locations I'd like to travel to someday, the type of home I'd like to live in one day and of course, my favorite daydream was about the man I'd want to spend the rest of my life with. I was never able to see his face, but I knew he'd be kind and attentive. He'd laugh easily and love hard. He'd have a special smile that was only for me, and his entire face would light up whenever he saw me. I just wished I could find someone like him in real life.

I finished my run and returned to my apartment, stripping my sweaty clothes off as I made my way to the bathroom. I turned the water on in the shower and then stepped under the spray, letting the water wash away the sweat and the last of my tension. Grabbing the bottle of soap, I poured a generous amount into my palm then began washing my body.

My fingers glided easily over my slick skin as I lathered it with soap and I sucked a breath of air between my teeth as my hand moved over my cock. It jumped in my palm and I wrapped my fingers around my shaft. I gave it a few pumps, but then forced my hand away before I could go too far. It had been way too long since I'd gone out and had any fun, but I had plans for that night and none of them included having an orgasm at my own hands.

After moving to California, I'd wanted to learn everything I could about my sexuality. I started going to gay bars and nightclubs and I found it surprisingly easy to pick up men. I began taking men home with me and I learned all kinds of things about my body and how best to please my partners. One night a friend of mine invited me to go to a swap party with him. I didn't know a lot about those types of parties, but I was intrigued so I said yes. That night had been eye-opening for me, to say the least.

Upon entering a swap party, one member from each couple dropped their car keys into a large glass bowl. Later in the evening, the bowl was passed around and the partner who hadn't dropped the keys withdrew a set of keys at random. Whoever the keys belonged to was who you spent the rest of your evening with. Of course, if I drew a woman's set of keys, I politely declined, and she'd find someone else to play with. No feelings were ever hurt, and no one was ever left out. Everyone knew that it was anything goes at those parties and I'd seen everything from heavy make-out sessions in dark corners to full-on orgies with bodies spread out all around the room.

Swap parties were a virtual smorgasbord of sexual delights, drawing an eclectic crowd of singles and couples, gay, straight, bisexual, and transsexual individuals. My friend had told me that they were the perfect way to discover more about my interests, and I certainly did. I'd always bottomed before that night, taking on the role that my partners had assigned me. However, I discovered that I was actually a switch. I still loved bottoming, but there was nothing like making a man, bigger than myself, beg for his release as he writhed beneath me.

With a frustrated groan, I rinsed off and climbed out of the shower. I quickly brushed my teeth and then went to my room to figure out what to wear. I sifted through my wardrobe before finally settling on a dark pair of designer jeans and a lavender button-down shirt. After getting dressed, I scrutinized myself in the mirror, turning around so I could check myself from all sides. The waistband of the jeans rode low on my hips and the soft denim hugged my ass perfectly. The shirt was a size too small, allowing the material to show off my firm, flat stomach. I may not have been very muscular, but I worked hard on keeping my body sleek and tight.

Happy with my outfit, I set to work styling my hair. I squirted a dollop of gel in my palm and then worked it over the strands of hair with a practiced hand. Next, I added a line of kohl under my eyes and just a touch of blush to my cheeks. Finally, I smoothed a bit of gloss over my lips and smacked them together. Satisfied with how I looked, I grabbed my keys and headed out.

My phone rang as I drove through the city and I rolled my eyes as the dash displayed Korey's name. I considered ignoring it, but I knew he'd just continue calling until I answered. Keeping my eyes on the road, I pressed the button on the steering wheel to connect the call.

"What's going on, Korey?"

"Hey! I wanted to go over next week's schedule with you. I'm about five minutes away so I figured I'd swing by and pick you up. We could go out, get a bite to eat maybe..." he said.

"I can't. I'm not home right now," I told him.

He paused for a moment, obviously surprised to discover that I wasn't just sitting at home. "Well, where are you? I'll come pick you up."

I struggled not to let him hear my exasperation. "It's Saturday night. I'm going out to have some fun and so should you. We've both been working way too hard and we deserve a little downtime."

"Downtime doesn't earn any money, Oliver." I frowned at his snippy attitude.

"Look, Korey. I appreciate how hard you work, and I know you're just trying to help, but there's more to life than just making money."

"I get what you're saying, Oliver, but in this city, pretty faces are a dime a dozen. You've got to work your ass off just to stay relevant. You know that old saying 'Out of sight, out of mind'? It's very true. If your face isn't being splashed on every magazine cover, then people will start to forget who you are, and they'll move on to the next big thing," he explained.

"I know how things work. I'm very aware how quickly I shot to the top and that it can all be taken away tomorrow, but I need this." I didn't bother to tell him that it had been three months since I'd gone out to a party or club. Three whole months since I'd gotten laid. It was none of his business and quite frankly, it was a depressing thought.

"Fine. Go have fun tonight, but I'm picking you up first thing in the morning, so we can discuss the schedule." His stern tone reminded me of my father's and my grip on the steering wheel tightened.

"See you in the morning," I said through clenched teeth, barely swallowing my frustration.

I ended the call and let out a deep sigh. Korey and I needed to have a serious conversation and soon, but I couldn't blame him for everything. We'd been on a mission the last few years, working our asses off to get me to the top. The problem was, the higher I climbed, the more I wished I had someone there to share it with. I'd tried to ignore it at first, but the truth was, I was lonely.

I hadn't changed the plan entirely. I still wanted to be on the cover of magazines, maybe one day even be the face of a leading cosmetic line. But there had to be more of a balance between my personal and professional lives. I definitely needed to talk to Korey, but it would have to wait. It was time to have fun.

I switched the radio on just as the DJ was finishing a breaking news report about the body of a young man being found off of the Santa Monica Pier. He was only twenty-one years old and had been strangled to death. I shook my head as I flipped to a different station. The crime rate in a big city was one thing I would never get used to after growing up in a small town. Pushing aside the depressing news and my conversation with Korey, I let the music settle over me.

My pulse sped up as I pulled into the long driveway of the house where the party was being held. Anticipation raced through me as I got out of my car and walked up the front steps. There were people milling around inside the spacious living room, talking in small groups and getting to know one another, but a look through the large sliding glass doors told me that most of the guests had gathered outside. It was a beautiful night, so I made my way over to the doors and stepped out onto the large concrete patio.

More people mingled around an enormous in-ground pool,

enjoying the warm evening air. Some were clustered around small tables, and a few swayed to the music being pumped through strategically placed outdoor speakers. Several heads turned, eyes traveling over me approvingly as I wandered around to the opposite side of the pool to the bar.

I ordered a cocktail then turned my back and rested my elbows on the bar as I waited for my drink. Looking out over the party, I could see Gabrielle, a woman I recognized from other parties and our hostess for the evening, winding her way through the guests, holding a large glass bowl. She smiled and chatted with everyone as, one after another, people dropped their car keys into the bowl.

The bartender handed me my drink and I took a sip. It was a fruity blend of pineapples and strawberries and it tasted cool and refreshing, the flavors bursting on my tongue. A server came by, holding a tray of delicate finger foods, but I waved her on.

I found a seat, tucked into a corner and sat down so I could observe my surroundings and see who was new to the scene. My eyes roamed over the party guests. It was an eclectic group, with people of all ages and ethnicities. Several faces I recognized from other parties we'd attended. Some looked at me with recognition, either from the same parties or from magazine covers, but I didn't worry about anything getting out to the tabloids. Everyone attending those parties understood that what happened at a swap party, stayed at the swap party.

I sipped my drink slowly as my eyes wandered over the guests, wondering which one I'd end up with that night. I had just set my glass down when a couple I'd never seen before walked through the doors. The man was tall and gorgeous with thick, jet-black hair. He was dressed in black slacks and a gray, short-sleeved polo shirt that accentuated his broad shoulders and tapered down to a trim waist. I felt the first stirrings of interest I'd had all night and I sat up a little higher in my seat, trying to keep track of the couple as they moved through the crowd.

They walked around the pool, drawing nearer to where I sat. The man kept his hand at the small of the woman's back, but the gesture seemed more comfortable than possessive in nature. I was curious about their relationship. They'd obviously arrived together, but something about their body language suggested that their closeness was more that of old friends than lovers.

A loud squeal drew my attention and I watched them turn as Gabrielle went running up to them. She and the woman obviously knew each other because they hugged. The man stood awkwardly as the woman introduced him to our hostess. Gabrielle offered him her hand and he shook it gently as she ran her eyes up and down him appreciatively. She said something that made the woman laugh and had the man lowering his gaze to the ground, an adorable blush spreading over his face.

I smiled, feeling completely charmed by the fact that he didn't seem to realize his appeal. As if he sensed that he was being watched, he turned his head and I sucked in a sharp breath as I suddenly found myself staring into the most mesmerizing pair of sky-blue eyes I'd ever seen in my life.

FIVE

Samuel

My fingers ached from gripping the steering wheel so tightly and I forced myself to loosen my hold. Soft laughter came from the seat beside me and I glanced over to see Gayle staring at me.

"I can't remember ever seeing you wound so tightly. Well, except for the night Brooklyn was born. You were so stressed out, I thought the doctors were going to have to sedate you," she said.

"I wasn't quite that bad," I insisted, rolling my eyes.

"Uh, yes, you were. At one point, the nurses forgot all about me because they were too busy getting you a drink of water and a chair, so you could elevate your feet," she argued.

"You have no idea what it was like. It was a very traumatic experience," I explained. I tried to hide my smile, knowing I was getting her riled up and enjoying every second of it.

"Are you kidding me?" she gasped. "You don't think it was traumatic for *me*? Try shoving a watermelon through a toilet paper tube and then we'll tal..." Her voice trailed off when she saw my shoulders shaking and I burst out laughing as she punched my arm.

"You did that on purpose, jerk!" she exclaimed, but her own

laughter took the bite out of her words.

I reached over and took her hand, linking our fingers together. "Sorry, I couldn't help myself. You know I think you were incredible that night. I did panic for a little bit, but then I saw how calm and in control you were, and it helped to calm me too."

"I was only able to stay calm because you were there." She grinned at me when I gave her an incredulous look. "It's true. You may have freaked out at first, but I knew you wouldn't let anything happen to either one of us. It's been that way throughout our entire marriage. You've always been my rock." Her voice shook a bit at the end.

"Thank you for saying that. I never wanted to let you down," I said sincerely.

"You never let me down, Sam, and I meant what I said. You have been the best husband anyone could ask for. You just were never meant to be mine." She squeezed my hand then let go as we drove for several miles in silence, each of us lost in our own thoughts.

I knew she was right. We weren't meant to be together, at least not forever. I was glad that being honest about our feelings hadn't damaged our friendship. Gayle had always been an important part of my life and I didn't want to lose that. Plus, we had Brooklyn to consider.

We'd decided that for the time being, we wouldn't mention our separation to our daughter. She was just beginning to settle into a new school, in a city far away, and we didn't want to hinder her progress. We needed this time for ourselves as well, to figure out what it was that we each wanted in our lives. Once we knew that, we would sit down together and explain things to Brooklyn, so she'd understand that neither of us were hurt by the decision and that we would always remain friends. Most importantly, we would explain that nothing could ever change our love for her or the joy we shared over being her parents.

"Are you sure you're ready for this? I know I kind of sprang it on you, but I didn't mean to pressure you into moving too fast," she offered, concern written all over her face.

"No, I'm sure. You didn't pressure me at all," I assured her. Out of the corner of my eye, I could see her shoulders relax and I was glad. I knew if I told her how nervous I really was, she'd insist on turning around and heading back home, but that wouldn't be right for either one of us.

"Who's hosting the party?" I asked, trying to change the subject.

"Gabrielle Sinclair. We've worked in the same office for years and we've become pretty good friends," she explained. Gayle had gone back to school once Brooklyn started kindergarten, quickly earning her degree and becoming a licensed attorney. She'd worked part time as our daughter grew but had recently begun working full time. Her enthusiasm was evident whenever she spoke about the work she was doing.

Checking to be sure the address was correct, I pulled into the driveway of a spacious home and parked behind a row of cars. I cut the engine but made no move to get out of the car. Gayle's nerves seemed to have finally caught up to her because her face had paled, and she sat staring out the window. Her hands repeatedly smoothing over her black dress, a sure sign that she was nervous.

"You're the most beautiful woman at the party," I told her.

Her head whipped toward mine in surprise. "How can you say that? You haven't even seen who else is here yet."

I shrugged my shoulders. "Doesn't matter. You'll always be the prettiest lady in the room," I answered simply.

"Charmer," she said as she bumped her shoulder against mine. A smile lifted the corners of her mouth and I was happy to see some of her earlier confidence returning.

"Hang on a second," I said as she reached for the door handle. She turned to me with an expectant look. "Take this," I said, pulling my wallet out of my back pocket.

"Thanks, but I've got money if I need to call a cab to pick me up."

"That's good to know, but this is something different," I told her. Her eyes widened when she saw the foil square I pulled from my wallet.

"You got me a condom?" she asked, blushing wildly.

"Hey! Safety is important and it's not just the man's responsibility to be prepared. A woman needs to make sure she's got protection," I informed her, giving her a stern look.

"You're absolutely right and that's actually very thoughtful of you. Thank you for watching out for me, Sam."

"Always," I responded. She smiled at me and I smiled back. *We are going to be just fine.*

That became my mantra as I forced myself out of the car and into the house. I was surprised at how many people were there. I'd expected the party to be small and intimate, with maybe only a few couples. It was quite shocking to see nearly thirty people there, and I wondered idly if there were enough bedrooms for everyone.

"This is nice," Gayle said, turning to smile at me as we stepped out onto a backyard patio with a large pool.

"Yeah. Everyone looks so…normal," I agreed.

Gayle laughed. "What were you expecting? Did you think everyone would be walking around with big red D's painted on their chests for deviants?"

I started to respond, but a loud shout had me whipping my head around in time to see a woman with long blonde hair running straight toward us, her arms stretched open wide. I took a step back as she neared and threw her arms around Gayle. They hugged and then Gayle turned, gesturing to me.

"Sam, this is my friend Gabrielle. Gabrielle, my husband, Sam."

"It's a pleasure to meet you," I said, taking her offered hand and shaking it.

"Oh, aren't you handsome. I may have to dig through the bowl and pull your keys out for myself tonight," she purred, batting her lashes at me.

Gayle laughed as my face flushed hot and my eyes dropped to the ground. I wasn't used to such brazen attention being given to me and my stomach knotted as I wondered just what I'd gotten myself into. Thankfully, the two women began chatting, saving me from having to respond. Wishing I had a drink in my hand, I turned my head toward the bar.

My eyes landed on a man seated alone at a table. He looked to be in his early twenties with stylish blond hair and cheekbones that would make any model jealous. He had a beautiful smile which widened as he held my gaze and I felt the strangest stirring in my gut when his tongue darted out, wetting his lips.

"Sam?" Gayle said, laying a hand on my arm. I jerked my head in her direction.

"I'm sorry, what?" I asked, feeling flustered.

"Gabrielle asked if you wanted to put your keys in the bowl," she repeated, her brow furrowing with concern. "Are you alright?" I glanced over and saw Gabrielle watching me closely. She was holding a large glass bowl, filled with various sets of car keys.

"You don't have to participate, if you don't want. Lots of couples prefer to just observe their first time," she informed me kindly. I appreciated the offer and, while part of me wanted to take her up on it, another part of me knew that if I didn't go for it now, I might never talk myself into coming back again.

"No, I'm fine," I assured them both then I slid my keys from my pocket and without another thought, dropped them into the bowl.

I glanced over my shoulder, wondering if the man was still watching, but found his table empty instead. I wasn't sure why that made me feel disappointed, but I didn't have time to think on it further because Gayle suddenly grabbed my hand and led me back into the house.

We ordered a couple of drinks then wandered back outside and found a place to sit. A few other couples joined us, all of them friendly and outgoing. It was apparent that they all knew each other very well and I ventured to guess that this wasn't their first swap party. When they learned that it was our first time, they went to work trying to put us at ease. I appreciated the gesture and I could see Gayle relaxing next to me.

One man in particular seemed quite interested in Gayle and he began openly flirting with her. I was on alert in case she needed me, but it quickly became clear that she was enjoying the attention. I waited, expecting it to seem strange to see my wife flirting with another man, but I found myself smiling instead at the happy glow to her cheeks. There was no reason for me to stand guard. Gayle was exactly where she wanted to be.

After a half hour or so, I excused myself to go to the bar for another drink. Gayle hadn't wanted anything else, so I stood there with my arms folded on the counter as the bartender poured me a rum and Coke. Someone moved in close beside me and I heard a soft voice order a vodka and cranberry. Chills raced over my skin and I knew before I even turned my head that it would be him. The beautiful blond that I'd caught looking at me earlier.

"Is this your first swap party?" he asked.

He was even more breathtaking up close with his flawless skin, plump lips the color of wine, and painfully long lashes that framed the most remarkable chestnut-colored eyes. He was extraordinary. He gave me a strange look and I realized I'd completely ignored his question, staring at him for several seconds with my mouth hanging open. I wasn't even sure I'd breathed. He probably thought I was a complete moron.

"Umm...is it that obvious?" I finally responded lamely. His lips curled up in a soft smile and my stomach flip-flopped all over itself.

"No, I just haven't seen you at one before...and I'm pretty sure I would've remembered if I had," he told me, looking up at me through his thick lashes. I felt my face heat up when I realized he was flirting with me and his smile grew when he saw my blush. I searched for something to say, but everything about the man had me feeling off balance.

"What's your name?" He moved in closer and I could smell a hint of cologne. It was a clean, masculine smell, not at all like the perfume Gayle always wore. My cock twitched inside my pants and I had the overwhelming urge to lean in and bury my nose in the crook of his neck, inhaling his intoxicating scent until I was dizzy.

"Samuel. Well, friends call me Sam," I answered.

He slid his hand between our chests and held it up to me. "It's very nice to meet you, Samuel. I'm Oliver." I held his gaze as I slipped his delicate hand into mine. A quiet thrumming, like the feel of a butterfly's wings, danced across my skin as our hands connected for the first time. He made a small sound, almost like a squeak and his eyes widened a fraction of an inch.

The butterfly effect suddenly popped into my head. It was the belief that a single butterfly, flapping its wings, could cause a series of events to occur, eventually leading to a hurricane. I'd always scoffed at the idea, but as I stood there, holding on to Oliver's hand, I suddenly believed that something small could indeed have lasting effects. I wasn't likely to forget meeting this man anytime soon.

He seemed flustered as he reached for the drink the bartender had set on the counter. He started to leave, but then stopped and turned to face me. "Enjoy your first party, Samuel. Hopefully I'll see you around." With that, he turned and walked away.

There was a slight tremble to my hand as I reached for my own glass and I picked it up carefully. I wound my way back to where Gayle was sitting and talking with another couple. She glanced at me as I sat down, then did a double take.

"Are you okay?" she leaned over and whispered.

"Yeah, I'm fine," I told her, bobbing my head up and down. I wasn't sure if I was trying to convince her or myself. All I knew was my heart was still racing from that brief encounter. She gave me a skeptical look, but the woman on the other side of her asked a question and she turned back around to answer.

I settled back in my seat, taking a healthy sip from my drink as the conversation flowed around me. Sultry music played in the background and the reflection of the strands of lights, strung across the pool, sparkled on the surface of the water. Patio heaters had recently been lit around the pool, warming the area just enough to ward off the gradually cooling night air.

I looked around at the other partygoers. As the night progressed, the feel of the party had shifted from a casual get-together, to an exhilaration that traveled throughout the guests like a steady vibration. Men and women eyed each other in an obvious show of interest and hands began lingering intimately on the arm of the person sitting next to them.

My eyes wandered around the outdoor space, taking everything in. The drink I held in my hand was helping to take the edge off. My earlier nervousness had been replaced with curiosity. Many of the couples I saw seemed very happy together, a few of them even wore wedding bands and I wondered what had drawn them to a party such as this. Were they in open relationships or did they prefer to play with others within the committed relationships they had formed? Perhaps there were others like Gayle and myself, who had come as friends, searching for something new.

Without meaning to, my mind drifted to Oliver. Who was he there with? Was he in a committed relationship? Married even? If so, was it with a man or a woman? The spark of interest in his eyes had me thinking he was gay or at least bisexual. I swallowed hard at the thought. My thoughts were interrupted though as Gabrielle called for our attention. Heads turned to watch the beautiful blonde as she stood in the center of the patio. She smiled at all of us.

"Welcome, everyone. Frank and I are very excited to have you all here with us tonight." She gestured to a man off to the side who didn't bother to look up as he shared a heated kiss with a sexy redhead. "Apparently, Frank's ready to get this party started. Who's with him?" Gabrielle said with a laugh. Everyone clapped their hands, eager to get things moving.

"Okay, before we get to the fun, let's go over the rules to make sure everybody is on the same page, shall we?" A chorus of good-natured groans went up, but everyone listened all the same.

I gave our hostess my full attention, curious as to what kind of rules there were at a swap party. I soon learned that while there weren't many, the ones in place were there for a very good reason and if broken, you might be asked to leave the party and possibly be banned from attending any other swap parties in the future.

Gabrielle continued, her earlier playfulness turning serious. "The rules are as follows. Sex without condoms is strictly forbidden. You don't want to wear a condom, you don't get to play. There are no exceptions. Second, everyone is to be treated with respect. If you'd like to decline from playing with someone, that's your prerogative, but don't be a dick about it. Even the most gorgeous people deal with body issues so keep that in mind. On the flip side, be courteous if someone is telling you they aren't interested. No *always* means no!"

She paused, looking around at her guests to make sure they had all heard her. Satisfied that everyone was willing to comply, she smiled. "Okay then. Let's get this party started." A round of cheers went up and the music was changed to something with a sensual beat as Gabrielle began walking around with the bowl of keys.

I followed her with my eyes, my nerves kicking in as she made her way around the pool. Was I seriously going to do this? Would I be able to sleep with someone new that night? Regardless of the fact that Gayle and I weren't in love, neither of us had ever been with anyone else.

I'd never given it any thought over the years. Once I married

Gayle, I was fully committed to her. A part of me felt like I was betraying her, and I had to remind myself that we'd agreed to this. We weren't cheating on each other; our lives were just going in different directions.

Gabrielle stopped at the opposite end of the pool near a group of men and women and I saw a flash of blond hair move toward the front. I leaned forward in my chair and watched as Oliver moved in closer to Gabrielle. Slowly, the young man reached his hand in the bowl and grabbed a set of keys.

I couldn't see them well enough from that distance, but a flash of red on the keychain told me that they weren't mine and the breath I'd been holding suddenly whooshed out of my lungs. I wasn't sure whether it was relief or disappointment that caused my reaction. I wasn't even sure why I was reacting to him at all.

In eighth grade, I'd been surprised to find myself drawn to my English teacher. Mr. Lasseter had warm eyes and a kind smile and whenever he looked at me, I'd get a strange feeling in the pit of my stomach. I didn't understand at the time what it was, but as I got older, I figured out that what I'd been feeling was attraction.

Moving on to high school, I'd found other guys my age attractive as well and a part of me wondered if I might be bisexual. The people in my small town didn't exactly care for anyone who was different though, so I kept quiet. I'd planned on spending my time in college exploring my sexuality and figuring out just who I was. But then Gayle got pregnant and that was all pushed aside as I was forced to grow up, seemingly overnight. I'd shoved that part of myself completely in the back of the closet and tried to forget about it. That was, until I laid eyes on a very alluring blond.

I wasn't sure what it was about him that was bringing all of those old thoughts and feelings to the surface. Maybe it was because Gayle and I were no longer together and for the first time in years, I felt a sense of freedom. Perhaps it was because the man was breathtakingly beautiful. Whatever it was, it had me feeling completely off-balance, but not in an altogether unpleasant way.

I was pulled from my thoughts as Gabrielle made her way over to where we were sitting and held the bowl out to Gayle. Gayle turned to me with a questioning look in her eyes as if wanting to be sure that I was okay with the two of us moving on. I wanted this for her. For both of us. We'd been responsible, and we'd put our dreams and wishes aside to raise our daughter. We'd done all of that and we'd done it to the best of our abilities. That was finished though, and this was our time. We owed it to ourselves to figure out what would make each of us happy.

I gave her a reassuring smile and nodded my head once. She smiled back nervously then with a slightly shaky hand, reached inside the bowl and pulled out a set of keys. Her shoulders visibly relaxed as if that one single act had released a huge weight and her smile turned more genuine.

When everyone had been given the chance to claim a set of keys, Gabrielle announced that it was time to find our new play-mates for the evening. I hugged Gayle and whispered in her ear that she could text me if she needed me for any reason. She gave me a grateful look and then disappeared into the crowd of people that were wandering around in search of their match for the night.

I looked at the far side of the pool, trying to find Oliver, but I'd lost him. My attention was pulled back around when a woman came to stand in front of me. She was thin and sexy with black hair that hung perfectly straight and smooth to her shoulders. She was wearing a red dress that showed off her ample cleavage and matching red stilettos. The subtle smell of lilacs lingered in the air around her, but it failed to elicit the same response as Oliver's cologne.

"Someone told me these were yours," she said with a smirk, holding up a set of keys between her thumb and pointer finger and giving them a quick shake so that they jingled. My eyes zeroed in on them and I immediately recognized them as my own.

"Yes, those are mine," I told her, surprised at how calm my

voice sounded.

"Excellent. I saw you walk in here tonight and was hoping I'd end up with you," she purred. I was flattered by her words, but I didn't get a chance to respond before she grabbed my hand and started pulling me around to the other side of the pool.

SIX

Samuel

"**W**ould you like a drink?" I asked as we neared the bar. I didn't know about her, but I sure could use another one. My recent bout of anxiety had burned through the two drinks I'd already consumed. and I needed something to help take the edge off if I was going to make it through what came next.

"Sure," she said, flashing me a wide smile. She still held my hand as we walked up to the bar and placed our orders. Needing something strong, I got a whiskey while she chose a strawberry daiquiri.

I watched quietly as the bartender poured everything into a blender and began mixing her drink. I wondered idly how Gayle was doing. It was odd to think of her going off to have sex with another person, but it didn't bother me like I'd worried it might. I guess that was proof that we were really and truly over. Instead of feeling sad, I felt relieved to know that we weren't making a big mistake by being there.

"So, what's your name?" the woman asked, pulling me from my thoughts.

"Oh, um. It's Samuel, but everyone calls me Sam," I told her. I turned my head toward her. "And you are?"

"It's nice to meet you, Sam. I'm Carmen," she responded, stepping in closer to my side. I could feel the warmth of her skin through the thin layer of my shirt.

She ran a manicured fingernail up and down my arm and I swallowed hard. It had been so long since anyone had flirted with me and I was severely out of practice. Now, in the space of an hour, two people had flirted with me and my mind wasn't sure what to make of it. The bartender handed our drinks over just then and I gave him a grateful nod. I shoved a couple of bills into the tip jar before grabbing the glasses, then turned around to find a place for us to sit.

While many couples had chosen to go inside the house, others, like us, were enjoying the fresh air instead. We made our way over to a set of lounge chairs and claimed them for ourselves. I set our drinks down on the small table between the chairs then waited for Carmen to take a seat before sitting down.

Moaning off to my right caught my attention and without thinking, I turned in that direction. My eyes nearly bugged out of my head as I saw a couple, not more than a few feet away from us. The man was kneeling on the concrete with his head buried under the skirt of a woman who lay stretched out on a lounge chair with her knees bent. His fingers disappeared under the skirt as well and by the sounds she was making, she was very appreciative of the things he was doing to her. I cleared my throat and then turned back around to reach for my drink.

"Is this your first swap party?" Carmen asked.

A sense of deja vu came over me as I responded. "Is it that obvious?"

She chuckled. "Just a little. Your face turned bright red when you saw them. Don't you like to watch others having sex?"

I shrugged my shoulders. "I don't know. I've never done it. Unless you count watching porn, but I haven't even done that in several years." My face grew hot again with my admission.

"Trust me, porn is great, but live shows are always the best. Take what they're doing, for instance," she said, gesturing across the pool at three people who hadn't wasted any time getting naked. "It's sex in its rawest, most animalistic form. Nothing scripted or rehearsed. Just pure lust and forceful need driving them."

Carmen's tone had taken on a husky quality and I looked over at her as I finished taking a drink and set my glass back down. Her skin was flushed, and her fingers trailed over the thin gold necklace at her throat, slowly working the charm back and forth in an unconscious gesture. Her tongue darted out to wet her lips and her eyelids lowered halfway.

I turned my gaze back on the threesome who were sprawled out in a tangle of limbs. One woman was stretched out on her back, both legs spread wide and her knees hooked over the arms of the chair. A man leaned over her head pushing his swollen cock between her plump lips while the other woman buried her face in her pussy.

It was a very erotic scene, but my attention was drawn to an upstairs bedroom as a light suddenly flicked on. The window reached from floor to ceiling and allowed me and everyone else around the pool to see a good portion of the room. I watched as two figures walked into the room, kissing as they made their way closer to the window and I swallowed hard when I realized it was two men. A lamp flicked on next to the window, illuminating their bodies and keeping them from being in shadow.

One was tall, with short hair and the physique of a bodybuilder. I could see the play of muscles in his bicep as he halted their kiss long enough to reach over his shoulders and pull his shirt off over his head. With his torso on display, he was enough to make any person, gay or straight, sit up and take notice. But I barely paid him any attention as my eyes zeroed in on the smaller man he was with.

He had perfect, honey-colored hair and even with his back to me, I knew he had the warmest brown eyes and lips that begged to be kissed. My cock began to stir as I realized the show I was about to watch would be starring the one man who had been stirring things inside me ever since I first laid eyes on him.

Oliver.

As if he'd heard me thinking his name, he turned his head and looked over his shoulder. Right at me. My breath caught in my throat. *Had he known I was there? Was he putting on a show for everyone or was this all for me?* The wicked grin he gave me told me it was probably the latter and I had to bite back a moan.

He used his hands to maneuver Thor, as I'd begun to refer to the larger man in my head, so that their sides were facing the windows. I watched as Oliver looked up at him, running his palms up and over the man's massive chest. He said something to Thor which caused him to grab Oliver and kiss him hard and I felt a spark of jealousy that it wasn't *my* lips pressing against those perfect lips, it wasn't *my* tongue that was delving deep inside to taste his mouth.

My cock pressed painfully against the zipper of my pants as I watched Oliver's hands slip down between their bodies. He pulled the man's belt free then worked the button open and lowered his zipper. I stopped breathing as he reached his hand under the waistband of Thor's boxers and pulled his cock out.

Oliver gripped the man's erection in his hand and I gasped as if I could feel his slender fingers around my own aching shaft. Somewhere, in my sex-hazed brain, it began to dawn on me that I wasn't just imagining things. I was feeling actual fingers.

Confused, I looked down and was shocked to find Carmen kneeling next to my chaise, grinning up at me like the cat that got the cream. Even more shocking was the fact that I'd been so absorbed in watching Oliver that I hadn't noticed her undoing my pants or pulling my cock out. In fact, I'd completely forgotten she was there, but my brain seemed to have a way of short-circuiting whenever I saw Oliver. I looked around embarrassedly, but everyone was too engrossed in their own activities to care about what we were doing. Or rather, what Carmen was doing to me.

"You go on and enjoy that," she said, nodding her head toward the window. "I'm going to enjoy the hell out of this." Her eyes darkened as they looked back down at my cock.

I should have felt badly for not focusing more on her. I should've pulled her up my body and feasted on her lips. I should have been squeezing her ample breasts and licking her pert nipples. But one glance at the window and all of my attention was back in that room. Back on Oliver.

My heart hammered wildly in my chest when I found him watching me and when he saw that he had my full attention, he smiled; a sinfully wicked smile that promised so much more to come. Slowly, his tongue slid out and licked over his bottom lip and I visibly shuddered as goose bumps raced over my skin. I held my breath as I waited to see what he was going to do next. Fortunately, I didn't have to wait long.

Oliver grabbed the man's jaw and gave him a scorching kiss right before he lowered to his knees. I tried to hold myself steady as tremors of need began wracking my body. I'd never felt so on edge, so filled with anticipation, in my life. I couldn't even begin to imagine what it would be like if I were the one standing in that room with Oliver kneeling in front of me.

What would it be like to kiss another man? To feel a strong, tight body pressed against my own instead of the softer, curvier body I was used to. What would it feel like to have those plush lips wrapped around my cock, licking and sucking me and taking me down his throat? What would it be like to taste his cock in my own mouth? My cock began leaking as the desires I'd locked away for so long suddenly sprang to life, refusing to be ignored any longer.

Oliver's tongue swiped over the tip of the man's swollen cock, but he kept his eyes trained on me, making sure I was watching. I couldn't have looked away if I'd tried. He tongued a line up and down the length of the man's dick, worshipping it with his mouth.

Suddenly, he swallowed him whole just as a pair of warm, wet lips engulfed the head of my cock. My mouth fell open in a silent scream and my hands gripped the arms of the chair.

My eyes stayed locked on Oliver as my hands moved down on either side of the head that was bobbing up and down between my legs, gently urging her on. I noticed however that Thor wasn't holding back at all. He gripped the back of Oliver's head and held on as his hips thrust forward, sending his entire cock down the smaller man's throat. Oliver didn't seem to mind though. In fact, he began working the man's shaft with complete abandon and it took everything in me not to mimic their movements and shove my cock deep inside Carmen's throat. I was nearing the edge when she pulled off me.

I lay panting, trying to get myself under control, but my mouth went dry as the man hauled Oliver to his feet and began stripping him. Inch by delicious inch, Oliver's tight little body was revealed to me until every flawless part was on full display. He was absolute perfection and the desire to touch him, to feel all that silky skin beneath my fingertips was so sudden and so fierce that it stole my breath away. I'd never felt so physically drawn to another person.

Thor rid himself of the rest of his clothing and beside me, I could hear the faint rustle of clothes as Carmen stripped herself and then pulled my pants down my legs. Turning Oliver to face the window, the man ran his hands over Oliver's shoulders and down his arms, then lifted his hands and placed them one by one on either side of him so that Oliver's palms were pressed flat against the glass.

Oliver's cock stood strong and proud, the tip of it flushed and leaking as he stared down at me. His lids were heavy and the look in his eyes nearly had me coming right there so I reached down and wrapped my hands around my cock, gripping the base tightly to try and stave off my impending orgasm.

The man reached for something off to the side and I swallowed hard as I watched him open the bottle of lube and pour some out into his hand. Anticipation thrummed through my body and I bit my lip as he stepped in close behind the smaller man. Oliver's mouth dropped open as the man began touching him *there* and a growl rumbled up from deep inside my chest.

I needed to come, and I needed to come soon.

Oliver must have felt the same sense of urgency because he said something to the man that had him reaching for a foil packet and ripping it open with his teeth. I barely registered the feel of a smaller hand brushing mine aside, but then there were two hands sliding a condom down my length and my eyes shot to Carmen. I knew I should be doing something, giving her something, but I was torn as everything in me begged to look back at that window. As if she could read my thoughts, she chuckled.

"Just let go and have fun. I am," she assured me. I stared at her, looking for any signs of disappointment. Finding none, I turned my gaze back to the window. Back to Oliver.

He was staring straight at me, his legs spread apart, hands on the glass and his hips thrust back in invitation. I had never seen anything more glorious in my life. The man stepped in closer behind him and he wrapped one solid arm around Oliver's waist to secure him. With her back to me, Carmen moved to straddle the chair and slowly began to lower herself down.

Oliver's head dropped forward as the man slowly pushed his way inside. At the same time, a snug, wet heat enveloped the head of my cock and as it swallowed every inch of me, I imagined that it was Oliver's tight channel I was sinking into. His head shot up and as his eyes locked with mine, I wondered if he were imagining the same thing.

With graceful movements, Oliver began gyrating his hips, grinding them back on the other man who reached down and wrapped his beefy hand around Oliver's dripping cock. With a sense of urgency, I thrust hard into Carmen. She shouted her delight and began riding me even harder. My fingers grasped her tiny waist, but

I refused to look away from Oliver for even a second. I wanted, no, I *needed* to watch him come apart.

My balls tightened, and a flash of something white-hot traveled down to the base of my spine. "Come on, come on," I whispered desperately.

I could've sworn I heard Oliver shout from inside the house as his body convulsed and ribbons of cum spurted out the head of his cock, painting the window and dripping down the glass. It was enough to send me hurtling over the edge and I came with a roar, filling the condom as Carmen tightened around me, milking me of every last drop.

My eyes drifted shut as wave after wave of pleasure wracked my body. I felt Carmen lift off of me as I lay there, gasping for air. I pried my eyes open and looked at her, guilt slamming into me. She'd said she was fine with it, but I couldn't help feeling like I'd mistreated her in some way.

She smirked at me as she pulled her dress down over her head and began smoothing out the material. "I know what you're thinking, but don't feel bad. That man up there is my husband," she said, pointing to the window. "We like to watch each other having sex with someone else. This was just as much for us as it was for you guys."

"Oliver's your husband?" I yelped. I wasn't sure why that made my heart sink the way it did.

"Oliver? No, I'm married to Jared," she said with a laugh.

Relief swept over me as I realized she was talking about Thor and I laughed along with her. I stood on shaky legs and glanced up at the window, but there was no one there. Carmen leaned forward and kissed my cheek.

"Thanks for a fun evening, handsome. Maybe we can do it again sometime," she whispered, then she handed me my set of keys and walked back toward the house.

I retrieved my pants and quickly put them back on before

slipping into my shoes. Walking up to the house, I let myself in through the set of sliding glass doors. A group of people were having an orgy on the floor of the living room, but I ignored them as I made my way toward the front of the house.

Carmen and Thor...*Jared* were by the front door and I watched them share a passionate kiss before they opened the door and slipped outside, presumably to continue their evening in private. I pulled my phone from my pocket and brought up a car ride app then went outside where I searched the line of parked cars for any sign of Oliver. He was nowhere to be found though so with a sigh, I walked to my car and slid the keys up under the front seat then I shot a quick text to Gayle to let her know I'd left her the car to get home.

I strolled to the end of the driveway and stared up at the night sky as I waited for my ride. Even as I replayed every second in my mind, I found it difficult to believe that that had actually just happened. It was the single most erotic thing I'd ever done. And I wanted more. I wanted so much more.

SEVEN

Oliver

I stood off to the side, watching Kimi Forsberg's long, toned legs eat up the runway. Chin up, shoulders back, one foot in front of the other as she strode to the end, turned and headed back. One of the highest-paid models in the world, she was confident, fierce, and the epitome of professionalism.

I, on the other hand, had been distracted throughout the entire trip. It was fashion week in Milan and while it was usually one of my favorite weeks of the year, I'd found it nearly impossible to concentrate. A fact that hadn't gone unnoticed by Korey.

He'd shown up at my house bright and early the morning after the swap party with an egg white veggie omelet for me and a bacon and egg breakfast croissant for himself. I'd narrowed my eyes as he bit into his food, hating him just a little for being able to eat whatever he wanted.

We'd gone over my schedule, which included the trip to Milan as well as several photo shoots and a red-carpet appearance at the Emmy Awards ceremony. I watched in silence as each and every day of my planner was filled in with work-related obligations. The relaxed feeling I'd experienced since the night before vanished, replaced by tense shoulders and a feeling of dread. A headache formed at the base of my neck, throbbing its way upward and settling just behind my eyes.

Finally, I'd had enough, and I put my foot down. "I can't keep doing this, not at this rate anyway," I told him.

Korey looked at me as if he didn't understand a word I'd said. "What are you talking about?"

"This!" I exclaimed, pointing down at my tablet. "You have every minute of my life mapped out. When am I supposed to have any fun? How will I ever meet someone?"

"You meet plenty of people," he argued.

"Not people I want to date," I explained. "It's not even just that, either. I don't want to burn out, but I can feel myself heading in that direction. I want more time to myself in between jobs." Korey opened his mouth like he was going to argue, but the look on my face must've told him how serious I was.

"How much time are we talking?" he asked. I did my best to hide my smile, but inside, I was dancing.

"Not much. Just a few weekends here and there when we're not traveling."

"Fine. I suppose I can try to rearrange a few things," he sighed.

I jumped up from my chair and threw my arms around his neck. He seemed startled at first, but then he laughed, patting my back awkwardly.

"Okay, okay. That's enough," he said, pushing me back into my chair. "I'll switch around what I can and free up a couple of weekends, but you may have to do a couple of evening shoots to make up for that time. We can't lose focus and we can't lose momentum," he said sternly, pointing a finger at my chest.

I could've argued with him about that, but I decided to let it go for the time being. I'd won that round, and even though I could tell he wasn't happy about it, I was finally going to have more time to myself. I ate the rest of my breakfast with a smile as we discussed the magazine layout I'd be working on that week.

"Oliver, you're up," a young woman said, pulling me from my thoughts. She was wearing a headset and holding a clipboard in one hand and I recognized her as one of the show's coordinators. I'd met her earlier in the day but couldn't remember her name, so I simply nodded instead.

Pulling my shoulders back, I took a deep breath then stepped out on the runway. Lights flashed all around me as I sauntered down to the halfway mark, turned and jutted my hip out, eyeing the crowd as they looked over the new designs I was wearing. I started walking again, sharing a playful wink as I passed the other model sharing the stage.

I reached the end of the runway and made a complete circle before turning to make my way back. My steps faltered though as a man with thick, ebony hair, sitting in the front row caught my eye and my thoughts immediately flew to another man with hair like that. Hair I longed to run my fingers through.

Samuel.

I'd thought of little else since the swap party, and I blamed Samuel for my inability to focus. To say the events of that night had taken me by surprise would be a massive understatement, but it had been a good surprise. A very good surprise.

From the second he'd walked through the door, I'd been unable to take my eyes off of him. He was gorgeous, of course, and I caught more than one pair of eyes lingering over his broad shoulders and toned arms, his trim waist, and perfectly sculpted ass. He was older than me by more than just a few years, but he obviously took very good care of himself.

When he finally broke away from the woman he was with, I'd taken the opportunity to follow him to the bar and introduce myself. He was even better-looking up close, with a few streaks of gray running through the hair at his temples and the tiniest little creases just beginning to develop in the soft skin at the corners of his eyes. As I stepped closer, I caught a whiff of his cologne. It smelled woodsy and spicy and I took a deep, pulling the heady scent into my lungs.

There was something about the way he carried himself, the way he blushed when I flirted with him, that was so sweet and almost innocent. With my job, I was constantly surrounded by beautiful people. The difference between them and Samuel was, they all knew how attractive they were. The fact that Samuel seemed surprised that someone would take an interest in him was refreshing, to say the least, and it immediately sparked my curiosity.

He admitted that it was his first swap party and he looked a little uneasy about it, which made me wonder what had tempted him to go to a party like that in the first place. I was intrigued by him and I'd hoped I could spend more time getting to know him, but of course that wasn't how things turned out.

I was pleased to see I'd ended up with Jared though. He and I had fucked at a party once before and I knew he was a nice guy. I also knew that he was happily married, and he and his wife came to those parties as a sort of foreplay for themselves. They liked to watch each other having sex with other people and it gave Jared, who was bisexual, a chance to fuck other men. The fact that he wanted his wife and her partner for the evening to watch what we were doing played into my love of voyeurism, so all in all, we had a perfect setup that left everyone extremely satisfied.

As he led me through the house and up the stairs, he told me that his wife would be watching from outside by the pool. It wasn't until I stepped into the darkened room that I saw who she was paired up with. My heart took off, pounding a crazy, erratic beat in anticipation of what was about to happen, and I was more than ready when Jared flipped on the lights and began kissing me.

I put on the show of a lifetime, but in the back of my mind, I wondered if I'd pushed Samuel too far. I knew I ran the risk of running him off and never seeing him again, but I couldn't seem to stop myself. Relief mixed with excitement flooded my veins when I peered over my shoulder and found his eyes on me. The intense look he gave me told me that he wouldn't be walking away anytime soon.

The rest of the evening went by in a blaze of passion like I'd never felt before. He held my stare, neither of us looking away until Jared and his wife, and even the distance between us, ceased to exist. Every moan, every smell, every thrust deep inside my body felt as if it was coming from Samuel and the intensity of his gaze left me shaken to my core.

Reality came crashing in, right on the heels of the most powerful orgasm I'd ever had. I'd seen the ring on his finger as he'd shaken my hand earlier and I'd seen the beautiful woman he'd come to the party with. Samuel had come to play, but that was all it would ever be for him. It figured that the first time I met someone I was genuinely interested in, he was already taken.

I'd gathered my clothes and quickly put them on, barely tossing a goodbye to Jared over my shoulder as I raced from the room, down the stairs and out to my car. I'd chastised myself the entire ride home. I didn't know why I continued going to those parties. The men I met there were either already involved in a relationship or they were only interested in playing games. I couldn't blame them; swap parties had served their purpose for the past several years when all I wanted was a fun way to explore. But now, I was starting to want more, and I was crazy if I thought I'd find it there.

I'd promised myself then that I wouldn't go back, but my resolve began to crumble as the week went on and I couldn't stop thinking of Samuel. Memories of that night plagued me, and my work had suffered because of it. Not that anyone noticed, other than Korey.

He'd poked and prodded, wanting to know what had me so distracted, but I'd refused to tell him. I may never get to have Samuel the way I wanted, but the night we'd shared, the connection I'd felt with him, was special and I wanted to keep it all to myself.

I finished the rest of the show on autopilot and eventually made my way back to the changing area. Switching back into my clothes, I quickly grabbed my phone from my bag to check for any messages. My fingers froze over the screen though as I saw the unassuming app icon with a set of keys on it and the little red notification bubble in the top right corner.

I should've ignored the notification completely. I should've turned off my phone and put it back in my bag. I should've flown back home, curled up in my bed and slept for a week. There were many things I should've done. I opened the app instead.

My breath caught in my throat as I read through the message, naming a date, time, and location of the next swap party. One quick look at my watch told me that the party was the next day. Would it be so bad to go to one more? Maybe that was a one-time thing for Samuel and his wife and they'd decide to never go to another one. But what if he was there? And what if I got to talk to him? What if the connection between us was still there?

With a shaking hand, I pressed the *confirm attendance* button. My head fell back, and I stared up at the ceiling as I let out a long, slow breath. Had I just made a huge mistake? Was I only setting myself up for disappointment? I popped my head back up and gave it a quick shake. I was being ridiculous. There was a good chance that Samuel wouldn't even be at the party. If he wasn't, I could move on and continue my search for someone special. If he was there…well, I guess I'd cross that bridge when I came to it.

The flight was a long one with Korey eyeing me suspiciously from the seat next to me. Eventually, I'd grabbed my pillow and pretended to sleep so he'd leave me alone. I spent the rest of the flight questioning my decision to go to the party. By the time I got home I was exhausted, so I crashed into bed and slept for a solid twelve hours. My dreams were filled with images of Samuel, stretched out on the lounge chair, his blue eyes staring up at me as a head bobbed up and down between his legs.

I woke with a shout, cum spurting up my chest and wetting the sheets pooled around my waist. I immediately felt embarrassed. I hadn't had a wet dream since I was a horny teenager. I quickly stripped the sheets from the bed and started a load of laundry before climbing in the shower and washing away the travel grime and the cooling spunk from my chest.

After my shower, I went back to my room, noticing the time on the clock by my bed. I was going to have to hurry if I didn't want to be late. I grabbed a tight pair of red jeans and a thin, black silk shirt. A pair of black, high-heeled ankle boots and some diamond-studded earrings completed the ensemble. With a little eyeliner and some lip gloss, I was ready to go.

My stomach was in knots as I pulled into the driveway of the sprawling mansion where the party was being held. I could hear laughter and music coming from the backyard, so I bypassed the house and made my way around it instead. There were more people there than at the last party, but the house was also bigger which probably included more rooms to get lost in.

Feeling the need for some liquid courage, I made a beeline to the bar area and ordered a whiskey sour. I tossed it back quickly and then ordered another. The bartender handed it to me and I slid a tip in the jar before wandering up onto the deck. From that vantage point, I could see the entire yard and I let out a low whistle. Whoever lived there must have made some serious dough because not only was the house a mansion, but they had an Olympic-size pool with a natural stone waterfall. There was also an outdoor kitchen that would make Bobby Flay's mouth water and a large building off to the side which I wasn't sure if it was a pool house or a separate apartment. Perhaps for the hired staff?

My eyes traveled over the mingling party guests. I tried telling myself I wasn't looking for anyone in particular, I was just scoping out the night's prospects, but it was a lie and I knew it. There was only one face I was hoping to see that night. One pair of sky-blue eyes and one set of kissable lips that could curl up into the sweetest smile.

I nearly laughed out loud at my own ridiculous thoughts. I'd barely spoken two words to the guy before we were both off fucking other people. So, what was it about him that got me so hung up? There were literally thousands of other guys in the city whom I could get to know who weren't wearing a gold band on their finger.

I was about to turn and head inside, when laughter pulled my attention over to a group of people standing just to the left of a spacious flower garden. A man was talking, his hands waving in the air as he got carried away with his story while everyone else around him was listening with rapt attention. Everyone that was except one man whose head was turned, staring at me intently. His eyes widened when he saw that he'd been caught, and he quickly looked away.

I stared back at Samuel, willing him to turn my way. A few seconds later, I was rewarded when his eyes flicked over to where I stood. Holding his gaze, I gave him a slow, playful smile then held up my nearly empty glass, tilting my head in the direction of the bar. I held my breath the entire way down the steps and over to the bar, hoping that he'd take the hint and follow me over there.

It was only a matter of minutes before he moved in beside me at the bar. I looked up and suddenly felt tongue tied as his rich scent filled my nose and his blue eyes locked with mine. It was there, that low hum of electricity just underneath the surface of my skin. I'd only ever felt it once before, the night I met him.

"What can I get you to drink?" the bartender asked.

"I'll have a scotch, please. Oliver?" A low heat pooled in my belly at the sound of my name on his lips, spoken in that deep bass.

"A whiskey sour, please," I answered without looking away from him.

"You look amazing," Samuel said, then his eyes widened as if he hadn't meant to say those words out loud.

"Thank you. You look pretty good yourself," I said with a smile, even though that was the understatement of the year. He looked so much better than pretty good. In fact, he looked down right edible. I didn't think he'd take well to me saying that though. He was still too skittish and the last thing I wanted to do was scare him off.

A few moments later we had our drinks and began wandering around, looking for an empty place to sit and talk. There were no chairs available though and I wasn't about to let an opportunity pass me by to spend some time with the man who'd been haunting my every waking thought. I looked around, searching for a place where we could go.

I glanced up at the house and then scanned the yard one more time, my eyes landing on the darkened pool house. Without a word, I grabbed his wrist and pulled him behind me. Jiggling the handle of the door, I was pleased to find it unlocked and unoccupied.

I tugged him into the dark building and shut the door, separating the two of us from the noise and the crowd. We stood close to each other, our breaths mingling as we waited for our eyes to adjust to the sudden darkness. I realized I was still holding onto his wrist, so I let go, slowly, letting my fingers trace over his soft skin first. He drew in a sharp breath and I smiled into the dark. I reached behind me and turned the lock on the door. I finally had Samuel right where I wanted him, and I'd be damned if I was going to let him get away.

EIGHT

Samuel

"**W**atch your eyes," Oliver warned right before the lights flicked on.

It took my eyes a few seconds to adjust and then I looked around. It looked more like a small home than a pool house with the kitchenette, plush furniture, and large bathroom off to the side. All that was missing was a bedroom, I thought before I could stop myself. I glanced over at Oliver and saw him staring at me, a small smile playing at the corners of his perfect mouth.

"What were you thinking just now?" he asked. His voice was smooth as honey and it sent a ripple down my spine.

"Nothing," I lied. He tilted his head to the side.

"If you say so," he said with a wink, not sounding at all convinced.

I watched him as he walked around the room, looking at the framed photos hanging on the wall. His movements were grace-ful, almost fluid, despite the heels he was wearing. I liked his heels though, and I particularly liked what they did to his ass. That pert little ass that looked like it would fit perfectly in the palm of my hand.

My cock jerked in my pants with that thought and I quickly moved across the room and settled onto one of the oversized chairs before he could see the evidence of my desire. The tight clothes he was wearing had been wreaking havoc on my mind since I first spotted him standing up on the deck. Especially since I knew exactly what lay underneath those clothes. Now, locked away in a space, just the two of us, I worried that I was going to lose my mind.

I sipped my drink as he came over and sank down in the chair directly across from me. Oliver smiled at me as he kicked off his boots and curled his legs up under him, making himself at home.

"So, did you enjoy your first swap party?" he asked. I nearly choked on my drink as it went down the wrong way. I glared up at him through watery eyes, but he just looked at me, an innocent smile on his face.

"Just decided to go right there, did you?" I sputtered.

"Well, that *is* the thing we have in common, so far anyway. I figured it was as good a place to start as any." Oliver may have had the face of an angel, but there was nothing but pure devilishness shining in those big doe eyes.

I pursed my lips. Two could play at that game. "It was quite good actually. I saw some very interesting things."

His eyes lit up and he leaned forward in his seat. "Really? What kind of things?"

"Oh, you know, lots of kissing and touching," I told him.

"What else did you see?" he asked, biting his bottom lip.

Feeling bold, I answered. "People laughing and talking. All around me on the grass, near the pool…"

"And did you see anything else interesting? Perhaps inside the house?"

I shook my head. "No, my eyesight's not that good. I couldn't see that far away." His mouth dropped open and he looked confused, but then his eyes narrowed as he saw my shoulders starting to shake. I broke out in a laugh, unable to hold it in.

"Asshole," he muttered, but soon he was laughing with me.

"Tell me about yourself, Samuel," he said a few moments later.

"What do you want to know?" I asked, feeling more at ease now that the tension had been broken.

"I want to know everything," he said, leaning back in his chair.

"I'm really not that interesting," I told him.

"Now, see, I have trouble believing that."

"Why?" I asked.

"Because I only met you once and I haven't been able to stop thinking of you since."

I swallowed hard. I'd never known anyone as bold as he was. Part of me was shocked by it, but another part felt exhilarated. Just being near him reminded me of how I'd felt when I rode the roller coaster with Brooklyn the summer before.

"How about I shoot some rapid-fire questions your way and you answer them without thinking?" he suggested.

I grinned at him over the rim of my glass, took a drink and then set it down on the side table. "Okay, I'm game."

"Excellent!"

"IF…" I held my finger up in the air, halting his enthusiasm. "If you're willing to answer the same questions."

"Fair enough," he agreed. "Okay, let's start with some easy ones. Last name."

"Bishop," I responded. "Yours?"

"Hughes." *Oliver Hughes. Why does that name sound familiar?*

"Favorite food?" he asked next.

"Lasagna."

"Mmmm. Lasagna," he replied dreamily.

I laughed. "Is that your answer too or did it just sound good?"

"Both. I haven't had lasagna in ages. Gotta watch this boyish figure, you know."

"I don't think you have anything to worry about," I said

quietly. He stared at me for a long moment, my words settling over both of us.

"Thank you," he responded. I was sure he'd had many people tell him he was beautiful; how could they not? But he seemed almost shy hearing it from me and that made my heart do crazy things.

I cleared my throat. "Next question?"

"Oh, right. Umm. Where did you grow up?"

"A small town in Oregon. How about you?"

"Probably an even smaller town in Alabama," he chuckled.

"I thought I detected just a hint of an accent. How long have you lived in California?"

"About four years. Moved here right after high school," he said.

"Ahh. So, that would make you...twenty-two? Twenty-three?" I asked weakly.

He eyed me closely as he answered. "Twenty-two. I'll be twenty-three in December. Is that a problem?"

I stared at him, this man who had tilted my world on its axis with just one look. The man who had given me my most erotic adventure thus far, without even touching me at all. The man who I'd spent the last week thinking about every day and dreaming about every night and I realized that no, no, it didn't matter. I'd spent my entire life abiding by rules that others had set in place for me and trying to do what was right. But this was what Gayle and I had talked about. It was finally my time to find what was right for me and what would make me happy. Was it this man? I had no idea, but I certainly wasn't going to let our age difference stop me from finding out.

"No, it's not a problem at all. Not for me anyway. Is it a problem for you that I'm almost forty?" I was suddenly nervous that maybe he wouldn't feel comfortable with our age gap.

"Hmmm. Let's see. A mature older man who's well spoken, has a great sense of humor and is sexy as fuck? Yeah, I think I can manage," he teased. I felt blood rush to my face and he laughed a light, tinkling laugh. "Oh, yes. There's that blush I'm so fond of.

"All teasing aside, there's something I need to know, Samuel." My smile drifted away when I saw the serious look in his eyes.

"What is it?"

"Are you married?" I leaned back in my seat. "I'm sorry, it's just that I saw a ring on your finger when we met and now it's not there and I just want to be clear about things before..."

"Before?" I asked. My mouth suddenly felt as dry as the Sahara.

"Uh-uh. Answer my question."

"Okay. Yes, I'm still married...for now. Gayle and I got married young. We were stupid and careless, but we ended up with the most incredible daughter. We put everything else aside and raised her the best we could until recently when she went off to college. On the other side of the country, mind you," I told him. Oliver gave me a sympathetic smile, but stayed quiet, waiting to hear the rest.

"Anyway, Gayle and I had a long and very honest talk. We agreed that even though we love each other and always will, we're not *in love* with each other. She's my best friend, nothing more. I took my ring off after the first party and I'm in the process of finding a place to live, but we haven't told our daughter yet."

Oliver opened his mouth to say something, but I held my hand up to stop him. "It's not because we think we may change our minds, if that's what you're thinking. We haven't told Brooklyn yet because we wanted her to get settled into her new school and make some friends first. She has a lot of changes going on right now and we don't want to make things any more difficult than they have to be," I explained.

"I wasn't thinking that at all. I think you sound like wonderful parents and Brooklyn's very lucky to have you. What I was going to ask was if Gayle was the beautiful woman you were with at the last party?"

"Yes, that was her. It was actually her idea to go to a swap party.

Neither one of us wanted to join a dating app and we're not the type to hang out at bars. A client of hers invited us to the party so we went. It was a way to test the waters while having someone there as moral support."

"I love that. Gayle sounds like an amazing woman."

"She is," I told him.

"Well, I for one am very glad you came to the… Oh, crap!" He shocked me when he suddenly jumped up and ran to the window. I followed over to where he was as he pulled the blinds apart and peeked outside. "Dammit. You missed the bowl being passed around. I'm so sorry, Samuel. Everyone already paired off while you were in here talking to me."

Oliver was frowning when he turned around and it looked all wrong on his beautiful face. Without even thinking, I reached out and cupped his cheek. His skin was creamy and smooth and felt just as silky as I'd imagined it would. He stared at me with those big chestnut-colored eyes and a swarm of butterflies erupted in my stomach.

"I didn't miss out on anything. I'm exactly where I want to be," I whispered.

Oliver leaned into my touch as his hand came up, his long elegant fingers circling my wrist. His other hand came up and slid around the back of my neck, applying just enough pressure to urge me closer, while allowing me to escape if I wanted to. His tongue came out to wet his lips and I couldn't wait any longer.

For years, I'd waited to find out what it felt like to press my body against another man, to feel his strong arms wrapped around me and to taste his firm lips as they opened up to me. I had waited a lifetime for *this* moment, but I couldn't wait any longer.

I leaned down slowly at the same time Oliver raised up, meeting me halfway. His eyes fluttered shut and I had just enough time to register how long his lashes were and the feel of his breath against my lips before we came together in the sweetest, most tantalizing kiss I'd ever shared. He made a sound in the back of his throat, somewhere between a whimper and a purr and I felt something inside me fall into place.

Everything I'd ever imagined this moment would be, everything I'd ever dreamed of, fell short of the reality of kissing Oliver. He wrapped his arms around my shoulders, pulling me in closer. His tight little body wasn't at all what I was used to, but it fit against mine like it was always meant to be. His lips were soft and warm, and my legs began to shake as his tongue swiped over my bottom lip, urging me to open to him.

My arms went around his waist and my hands slid up and down his spine, feeling the taut muscles in his back and the warmth of his skin seeping through the thin layer of his shirt. I felt the first sweep of his tongue against my own and my body felt like it was going to burst into flames. Someone moaned. It might have been me, but I couldn't be sure because my head felt dizzy and my skin felt too tight. Neither of us were in a hurry to end the kiss, but an unexpected rumbling had me pulling back. The look on Oliver's face was pure mortification and his head landed on my chest.

"I'm sorry. That's so embarrassing. I didn't have time to eat today," he said, his voice sounding muffled as he spoke into my shirt. I pulled away from him, so I could see his face. His lips were wet and swollen and it took everything in me not to haul him back in for another kiss.

"Why didn't you eat today?"

"I just got back from a business trip this morning. I was so tired, I fell asleep right away. When I woke up, it was getting late, and I didn't want to miss…" His eyes widened, and his words trailed off as if he hadn't meant to say that much.

"You didn't want to miss what?" I urged.

"You," he answered. I felt like my smile was going to split my face in two, so I leaned in and gave him another kiss instead.

"I would've waited for you," I whispered in his ear. He shivered against me and started to pull me in for another kiss, but his stomach made another noisy plea just then.

"Alright, get your shoes on," I told him. "I'm taking you to get something to eat. That is, if you're comfortable with that." Oliver nodded his head without any hesitation then he brushed past me as he walked over, sat down and began sliding his boots on.

"I can drive us, if you want. I never bothered to drop my keys in the bowl," he admitted shyly.

"That's okay. Neither did I." I held mine up, so he could see them, and we exchanged grins. No one paid us any attention as we slipped out of the pool house and around the side of the house to where the cars were parked.

We drove through In-N-Out Burger and I ordered burgers, fries, and chocolate milkshakes for each of us then I drove to a nearby scenic lookout and parked. We sat on the hood of my car and looked out over the glowing lights of the city. Oliver's eyes were as wide as saucers as I opened the bags and began handing him his food.

"Is this okay?" I asked him.

"Yes, of course. I just don't normally get to eat stuff like this."

My brow wrinkled in confusion. "What do you mean?"

"My job requires me to eat as healthy as possible," he said with a shrug.

"Oh, I'm sorry." I felt like an idiot and began gathering the food back into the bag, but Oliver pulled his arm back, holding his fries out of reach.

"Don't you dare be sorry and don't even think about taking these away from me unless you want to lose a hand," he warned.

I looked at him, startled as he popped a few fries in his mouth for good measure then we both started laughing. He grabbed the bags out of my hand and finished laying our food out between us as he explained that he was a model. I suddenly realized where I'd heard his name before and his eyes lit up when I told him that I'd heard my coworkers talking about him before over lunch, saying that he was the next fresh face in fashion.

We continued talking well after we were finished eating. He told me about the different places he'd traveled for work and I told him about Brooklyn and my work at the ad agency. The sun was coming up when I finally drove us back to the party, so he could get his car. There were still a few cars in the driveway, but most of the guests had gone home. Gayle had insisted on calling an Uber, saying that it was only fair since I'd done it last time.

As I pulled up alongside his car, Oliver pulled out his phone and asked for my number. I gave it to him and a few seconds later, my phone chirped in my pocket.

"Now you have my number too. Just in case you want to call or text," he said with a shy grin. Then, he leaned over the armrest and kissed me.

I was still smiling as he slid out of the car. I made it until he climbed into his own car before I was scrambling for my phone and bringing up the text from him.

Thank you for an unforgettable evening. I'm already looking forward to the next one.

My mouth tingled from the feel of his lips and my mind went over each and every perfect detail of that night as I drove home. Oliver was even better than I'd imagined after seeing him at the first party and I felt a bit like a teenager, knowing I'd be counting down the minutes until I could see him again.

NINE

Oliver

I t had been two weeks since my somewhat date with Samuel and I was still floating on cloud nine. I'd hoped to see him again right away, but I'd flown to New York two days later to do a fashion show and an interview on Good Morning America, where Robin Roberts asked me what it was like to be the fresh face of men's fashion. I must have said the right things because she called me charming and invited me to come back again. Korey was so happy he even stopped to buy me a slice of pepperoni pizza as we walked around, enjoying the sights.

The following week had been filled with one photoshoot after another. It was long and exhausting, but I couldn't complain too much since Korey had stuck to our agreement and not scheduled anything for that weekend. All I had to do was get through the next few hours and I'd be free for an entire two days.

Samuel and I had texted each other nearly every day since our night together and we'd even managed to call a couple of times at night. Each time, we'd stayed up talking until one or both of us fell asleep. He was a very special man; funny and caring and extremely intelligent. I'd never met anyone who I connected with so quickly and so completely. Even the differences between us, like our ages or our jobs, didn't carry much weight once we got to know each other.

I heard my phone beep from across the room and quickly tied the belt around the waist of the plush terry cloth robe Ben had given me. Luckily, we were on a break and Korey and Ben were busy discussing, or rather arguing over, how the next series of shots should go. I rolled my eyes at the two of them and left them to hash things out while I hurried over to my bag. I pulled my phone out and smiled when I saw it was a text from Samuel.

Samuel: *I agreed to go to the swap party tomorrow night. I wasn't going to, but Gayle asked if I'd go with her one more time. Personally, I think she's met someone she really likes and that's what's making her so nervous. Will you be there?*

Me: *Why weren't you going to go?*

Samuel: *Because I was hoping to spend time alone with you instead.*

Me: *Good answer. I'll see you there, Samuel.*

I started to put my phone away, but a second later, my phone chirped again.

Samuel: *Why do you call me Samuel? Everyone else I know calls me Sam.*

Me: *Oh, sweetie. Don't you know by now? I'm not like everyone else.*

Samuel: *Thank God for that.*

"What are you smiling about?" I looked up from my phone to find Korey standing over me. His arms were crossed, and his eyes were narrowed.

"Just talking to a friend," I told him, tucking my phone back inside my bag.

"Well, if it's the same 'friend,'" he said using air quotes, "that's been distracting you all week, then you might want to tell him that you're on company time right now and you'll talk to him later, okay?"

I glanced over his shoulder. Ben was fiddling with his camera, but I was sure he'd heard every word. I was used to Korey's holier-than-thou attitude, and I was usually able to take it with a grain of salt, but I'd be damned if I was going to let him tell me who I could speak to or when. I stepped closer to him, lowering my voice so only he would hear.

"Listen to me very carefully, Korey. You may be my agent, but I don't work for you. If anything, it's the other way around. So, this company time you speak of, it's *mine*. I take my job very seriously. I work my ass off and do everything that's asked of me, but *no one* is going to dictate who I can talk to. That's where I draw the line. Are we clear?"

Korey's eyes had widened as I spoke until I was sure they would fall out of his head. I'd never stood up to him like that and he obviously wasn't sure what to do with it. I supposed some of it was my fault. I'd allowed him to do or say whatever he wanted for so long, never feeling like it was worth arguing about, but he'd hit a nerve when he spoke that way about Samuel and I wasn't going to put up with it.

He gave me a terse nod instead of answering and went back over to his corner of the room to sulk. I was sure I'd be getting the cold shoulder for a while, but I couldn't find it in me to care. With a sigh, I wandered back over to where we'd been working. Ben was busy swapping out some of the props on the elaborate beach set he'd made.

When I'd first started modeling, it had seemed strange to be shooting a summer line of clothing in the winter and vice versa. It had made sense though once Korey explained the process and the time it took to get those photos ready for the big summer magazine issues.

For this session, Ben had pulled out all the stops; hauling in an enormous pile of sand which he'd smoothed out over the entire area and added a large beach umbrella, surfboards, and even a picnic basket. I knew he would've rather taken the photos down on the actual beach, but it was a little too chilly for me to be out there wearing nothing but swimwear.

"Go ahead and take a seat on the towel and I'll arrange you how I need to in a minute. I just have to grab a different lens for this."

I peeled my robe off and set it aside, then reached down to adjust the swim trunks the magazine's wardrobe department had sent for me to wear. They were little more than dental floss disguised as swimwear, but it didn't bother me. I'd learned early on that modesty was a luxury models couldn't afford. There were way too many hair, makeup, and wardrobe people touching our bodies, adjusting and tucking things in they didn't want seen and sometimes even taping them down. None of it was sexual or inappropriate, it was all just part of the job.

I sat down on the blue and white beach towel and pulled my knees up to my chest, wrapping my arms around my legs. Ben had very thoughtfully turned the heat up inside his studio, but the temperature outside had dropped considerably, and I still felt a little chilly.

"I turned the temperature up a bit more for you," Ben said as he came over, setting his camera down on top of the picnic basket. "With any luck, we'll get Mr. Sunshine so hot, he'll decide to go for a walk or something," he joked. I glanced over in Korey's direction. He wasn't paying any attention to us as he fiddled with his phone, but his forehead was dotted with sweat and he reached up and ran a finger around the collar of his shirt, trying to catch a cool breeze no doubt.

"You're bad," I responded, but I couldn't hold back a tiny laugh.

"Seriously though, I was glad to hear you stand up for yourself," he said.

"Eh, Korey's not a bad guy," I told him. Ben gave me a skeptical look. "He's really not. He's done a lot for me. I wouldn't even be here if it wasn't for him. He just has to be reminded what my boundaries are sometimes."

"If you say so," he said, obviously unconvinced by my words. I let it go though. I wasn't sure what had led to the animosity between the two of them, but I didn't plan on getting anywhere near the middle of it.

"So, tell me about this guy." I smiled, thankful for the change in topic and also because it was impossible not to smile whenever I thought of Samuel. "Oooh! That good huh?"

I nodded. "It's still too early to tell, but so far everything is going great." Ben set to work adjusting my legs, my arms, my chin how he needed, picking up his camera now and then to see how it looked through the lens.

"He must be very special. Does he have a name?"

"Samuel," I breathed.

"Hold still," Ben chastised gently, readjusting my chin. I hadn't even realized I'd turned my head. I really did become distracted whenever I thought of him.

'Sorry," I whispered, making sure not to move again.

"Don't be. It's good to see you so happy. Just don't let that one ruin it for you," he warned, hooking a thumb over his shoulder in Korey's direction.

"I won't," I promised. And I wouldn't. I'd been with enough guys to know that Samuel was someone really special. Spending time with him was too important to me to let anything get in the way.

We finished the session a few hours later and Korey drove me home after. He was mostly silent the whole way, other than to remind me of my early photo shoot Monday morning. I watched him as he pulled away from the curb. Hopefully a few days apart would help him get over whatever snit he was in.

The next day was spent catching up on all the mundane chores I hadn't had time to do during the week. Grocery shopping, laundry, and cleaning my apartment took up most of the day and before I knew it, it was time to get ready for the party.

I took a shower and brushed my teeth, then grabbed the bags that were lying on the bed and began pulling items out of them. I'd made a quick stop to my favorite boutique while I'd been out running errands and bought myself a new pair of black jeans and a black top that fell off one shoulder. My favorite part though was the silver threads that ran throughout the material, making it shimmer in the light.

I finished getting ready and then checked myself in the mirror. Fortunately, my hair had behaved, and I was able to get it to stay in a perfect upsweep over my forehead. The draping neckline of my blouse accentuated the slender length of my neck and I smiled to myself, hoping it would drive Samuel crazy. A set of silver dangly earrings and pair of black stilettos completed the look and with a satisfied grin, I headed out the door.

Traffic took forever so the party was in full swing by the time I got there. People were spread out throughout the house, but a large crowd had gathered in the living room. I stood along the back wall, thankful for my heels so I could see better as I looked around for Samuel. I found him standing near an impressive baby grand piano.

He hadn't seen me yet, so I took the opportunity to admire his toned body and his thick black hair with that smattering of gray that made him seem so distinguished. He lifted his glass to his lips and I licked mine, remembering the feel of those lips pressed to my own. I noticed the slight scruff along his jawline and I shivered as I pictured it rubbing against my cheek, my neck, on the sensitive skin of my inner thigh.

He looked in my direction just then and our eyes locked together. A smile grew on his face and his eyes lit up like he was so happy to see me. I'd never had anyone react that way just from seeing me and it made me feel all warm and mushy. *Oh Lord, I've got it bad.*

Samuel excused himself and made his way through the crowd,

over to me. When he finally reached me, we both stood there, smiling as if we weren't sure what to do, but then he leaned in and gave me a hug. To anyone else we may have just been old friends who were happy to see each other, but I felt the way he held me a little too long and wrapped his arms around me just a little too tight... pure perfection. And my God, the way he smelled. I wanted nothing more than to stay wrapped in his arms all night.

We were interrupted though when the host announced that it was time to pass the bowl of keys around. Samuel tensed beside me as the bowl came closer and I was sure he was worried about how to excuse himself from participating without offending anyone. Our hands were down at our sides, out of sight from wandering eyes so I took his hand in mine and gently pressed my keys into his palm. He looked at me out of the corner of his eye and I gave him a wink. His fist closed around my car keys, holding them tight.

A moment later, the host stopped in front of us and held the bowl out, rattling it around playfully. Samuel hid the set of keys as he reached inside the bowl and pretended to swirl his hand around. Seconds later, he pulled out his hand and held my keys up with a victorious smile. I had to bite the inside of my cheek to keep from laughing at his show. The host thrust the bowl in my face next, but I was ready for it. I pulled my phone out of my pocket and held a finger up in the air, giving the man an apologetic look.

"I'm so sorry. I have to take this call. I'll only be a sec, but you go ahead, and I'll choose later," I told him.

"Okay, don't forget. I'd love for you to get mine," he responded.

I felt Samuel bristle at my side as the man gave me a flirtatious wink. As he moved on to the next person, I heard Samuel mutter something about tossing the guys keys into the ocean and I couldn't hold back my smile.

Soon, everyone was pairing up and heading off in different directions. Samuel looked over the crowd to where Gayle was smiling and talking with another man. Satisfied that she was alright, we headed for the front door.

"I'm sorry about that. I just feel more comfortable knowing she's okay. Regardless of our marriage being over, she'll always be my friend," he said as we walked down the driveway.

"It's okay, really. I think I'd be a little worried if you didn't care so much about her," I told him, and it was the truth. I believed him when he told me that things were over between them and I respected the fact that they were able to stay friends. In the long run, their getting along would be the best thing for their daughter, for them, for everyone.

I reached out and took his hand. He looked down at where we were connected and then back up at me with a small smile, threading our fingers together. I led him over to my car, but he made no move to get in. My breath caught as he placed his hands on my hips and slowly backed me up against the side of the car. I could still see the bright blue of his eyes in the moonlight and when they swept over me, from head to toe. It felt like a caress.

"You look beautiful tonight," he whispered.

I wasn't sure which one of us leaned in first, but our lips met in a perfect kiss that started out sweet but grew progressively more heated until we were clinging to each other, each of us rock hard and gasping for air. I could've happily stayed like that forever, but I had other things I wanted to do as well.

"Come on, it's my turn to buy you dinner," I told him. He grabbed my wrist as I started to pull away.

"I believe these are yours." He was wearing a smirk as he held my keys up in the air. I reached for them, but he pulled his arm back, stealing another kiss from me instead. I was sure I was smiling like a loon when he pulled away, but I couldn't help it. I just felt happier when I was around him.

I drove us to a nearby steak place. It was just late enough that the restaurant wasn't crowded, and we were able to get seated at a small corner table. The lights were low, and a single candle was lit in the center of the table, giving off a romantic vibe. We talked over dinner, each of us enjoying a delicious meal. After the bill had been paid, we walked back out to my car.

"Do you need to get home right away?" I asked.

"Nope. I'm all yours." I knew he hadn't actually meant anything by it, but his words still struck a chord in me and hope bloomed inside my chest.

We drove down to the beach and I parked in a vacant lot. It was too cold to walk along the water, so we sat in the car instead, staring out at the silvery flashes as the waves crashed along the beach. I turned the car off but left the radio on low, so it was nothing more than background noise.

"There's something I've been wondering," I said hesitantly.

"What is it? You can ask me anything, Oliver." I turned in my seat, so I could look at him and he did the same, each of us resting our backs against the doors.

"Have you ever been with a man? You know, before Gayle?"

Samuel shook his head. "No. I was attracted to other guys growing up, but I knew better than to act on it in my small, backwoods town. Plus, being gay or bisexual wasn't accepted as easily when I was a teenager as it is now. One wrong move and I could've been beaten, or worse. Of course, I wasn't even sure that what I was feeling really was attraction because I liked girls too. It was all very confusing. I kept quiet for years, but the feelings never quite went away and when I went away to college, I figured I'd finally get the chance to find out."

I watched as he reached up and ran a hand through his hair. "Before I could get the chance though, I went to the party where I met Gayle and you know what happened after that. When I found out I was going to be a father, everything else just didn't seem to matter. My own needs were put on the back burner, as well as Gayle's, and we did what needed to be done to raise our daughter."

"Did you ever think about it though? Through the years?"

"Honestly, I tried not to," he admitted quietly. "I knew that something wasn't quite right, like I was missing a part of myself in some way, but I suppose I thought it just wasn't in the cards for me to find out, so I had to let it go. It was too painful not to."

"But then Brooklyn went to college," I said.

"Yeah. Brooklyn went to college," he repeated and the look on his face turned to wonder. "And here I am, being given a second chance to figure out who I really am. And then I met you…" His voice trailed off as I climbed over the console and straddled his lap.

"And I couldn't be happier," I told him right before my mouth slammed down over his.

My tongue swept into his mouth, dancing and swirling with his. My hips began to swivel, grinding my ass along his hardening cock and I swallowed the sexy groan that rumbled up from his chest. His hands slid around behind me and began cupping and kneading my ass until I thought I'd go crazy if I didn't get his fingers or his tongue or his cock inside me. However, I wasn't sure he was ready for all that yet and I didn't want to push him too far, so I decided to try something else instead.

"Please, Samuel, will you let me taste you?" I whispered. His pupils were blown wide and his breath blew against my lips as he stared at me, panting. He gave me a single, shaky nod and that was all I needed.

The windows were fogged up and the radio switched to a new song with a slow and sexy beat as I reached down for the lever and slid his seat back as far as it would go. His tongue darted out to wet his kiss-swollen lips as I sank to my knees on the floor. It was a tight fit, but I somehow managed, silently thanking Korey for talking me into starting those yoga classes a few years back.

I reached for his belt and quickly unbuckled it. I could see the rigid outline of his cock through his pants and I swallowed hard. I worked to undo his pants and slid them over his hips as his cock bobbed free. The head was a beautiful shade of red, the tip leaking as it reached almost to his navel. My mouth watered. Samuel had been very blessed, and I was about to partake in that blessing.

He hissed through clenched teeth as I wrapped my fingers around the base of his shaft then I looked up at him questioningly, wanting to be sure. He nodded once again, and I held his gaze as I lowered my head.

Samuel gasped at the first swipe of my tongue over his tip and I moaned as his salty, sweet flavor coated my tongue. His hand was shaking as he reached down and caressed my cheek. I slid my mouth around the head of his cock and began a slow and sensual bob up and down. My eyes were trained on him, wanting to see his reaction, needing to know if I pleased him. I got my answer when his head fell back against the headrest and his mouth dropped open in a long, low moan that seemed to come from deep within.

I continued that slow pace until his hand slid to the back of my head, pressing ever so lightly. I took that as my cue that he was ready for more and began to work my way down his thick shaft, swirling my tongue and hollowing my cheeks to create more suction. I took him deep into my throat, but I still couldn't take all of him. Using my hand that was wrapped around the base, I began stroking him, twisting my wrist on every upward sweep, using my saliva to slick my movements.

A burst of precum shot onto my tongue and my head swam with the delicious taste of him. He whimpered, a small, desperate sound as I pulled off of him, but then sighed as I lowered my head and swiped my tongue over his smooth sac. I gently pulled one orb into my mouth and then the other, swirling them around with my tongue and showing them proper attention.

I breathed deeply, drawing his warm, clean, uniquely Samuel scent into my lungs then I moved back up to resume my efforts with his cock. My own was aching by then, straining against my zipper and begging for attention, so I reached down and quickly undid my pants, freeing my cock and moaning loudly as I wrapped my fingers around the shaft and began stroking.

The vibrations of my moan must've done something to Samuel because he started a steady stream of dirty talk that had me hurtling toward the edge of an orgasm. I forced my hand to hold still, gripping the base of my cock almost painfully. I wanted to watch him come apart first.

When I was sure I had myself under control, I let go of my cock and slid my hand up under his shirt. My fingers explored the ridges and planes of his chest and abs, the slight fur on his chest tickling my skin. Samuel gasped as my fingertips found his nipple and began circling the tight nub. His hand clamped down on my wrist when I pinched his nipple gently between my fingers, but it was to hold me in place, not push me away.

Soon, Samuel began thrusting his hips upward, searching for more, urging me to go deeper, but I could tell he was holding back, not wanting to choke me. The guttural sounds coming from him let me know that he was nearing the end, so I doubled my efforts, sucking and swirling my tongue and taking him to the back of my throat.

A moment later, I felt his cock swell impossibly bigger and he let out a warbled line of curses as hot, thick cum shot down my throat. I watched him through it all and I had never seen anything more glorious; head thrown back and body tense, his face glistening with sweat as he rode out the waves of passion. Samuel Bishop was a sight to behold.

TEN

Samuel

I woke the next morning as the light, streaming through my window, landed on my closed eyelids, turning everything behind them a bright red. I kept my eyes closed and let the events of the night before replay in my mind.

If a person could die simply from pleasure, then I was sure I would've passed away right there in Oliver's car. The feel of his mouth wrapped around my cock, the things he did with his lips and his tongue; his hand stroking me in time with his mouth, all of it had come together to bring me the most powerful, most mind-blowing orgasm of my life.

And it was more than just finally experiencing what it was like to be with a man. It was being with Oliver himself, the way he seemed to know exactly what I needed and when to do it. It was as if we had been together forever and he already knew my body inside and out. It had taken many months of fumbling and asking questions before Gayle and I had hit our stride with each other. The fact that Oliver and I seemed to have skipped all that boggled my mind. Well, Oliver had anyway. I had yet to return the favor, but I wanted to. I wanted to very much.

THE SWAP

After I had come down from my high and could actually breathe again, I grabbed Oliver under his arms and hoisted him up in the seat with me. Seeing his pants already undone and his cock hanging out had my flagging cock trying to come back to life, but I ignored it and wrapped my hand around his long slender shaft instead.

He leaned up, his knees on either side of me and began gyrating his hips. It wasn't long before he began leaking, aiding in the movements of his cock through my tight fist. His hands held either side of my head as his mouth met mine in a wildly passionate kiss. I could taste the remnants of my release on his tongue and I was surprised by how much that turned me on.

Using my free hand, I quickly yanked his pants further down his thighs. Oliver looked at me with surprise and I froze, not sure if I'd crossed a line. A sensual smile spread across his face though and I let out a sigh of relief. He grabbed my hand and lifted one finger, pressing it to my lips until I opened my mouth and sucked it in, swirling my tongue around to wet it. Then he guided my hand to his crease.

"Please, Samuel. I need you to touch me," he pleaded breathlessly. He held my gaze, waiting to see what I'd do.

I knew what he was asking, but I was worried. Gayle had never been interested in anal play and I'd only allowed myself to explore my own a few times. What if I did something wrong? What if I hurt him? Oliver laid his forehead against mine, his beautiful chestnut eyes so open and honest. "Please, Samuel. You won't hurt me, I promise," he whispered.

My hand was shaking as I slid my finger between the tight globes of his ass. Oliver let out a moan as my hand drifted up and down through his crease, letting me know I was doing something right. The sound of his pleasure spurred me on, my movements becoming bolder until I was circling his puckered hole with the pad of my finger.

His hips picked up speed as they rocked back and forth, feeding his cock through my grip. His moans grew louder, and his head flung back, exposing his long graceful neck. The call of all that creamy white skin was too much to ignore, so I leaned forward, tracing its length with my tongue.

His movements started to become erratic and I knew he wouldn't last much longer so I gently bit down on the soft curve of his neck as I slid just the tip of my wet finger inside him. That set off a chain reaction within him and I watched, mesmerized as he arched his back, mouth hanging open in a silent scream. Cum splashed over my hand and up my arm and I took over, stroking him through his orgasm until I'd wrung every last drop from him.

Oliver was still trembling, but he lifted his head and watched me through hooded eyes as I lifted my hand to my face. I flicked my tongue out and took a tentative swipe then closed my eyes. It was both salty and sweet and even better-tasting because I knew it was *his*. I opened my eyes again and held his stare and he bit his lip to stifle a whimper as I continued licking my hand clean.

When I was finished, he threw his arms around me and crushed his mouth to mine, letting our flavors blend together until they were one. The need for air finally forced us to stop, but neither of us were willing to let go. We sat there in his car, parked on the edge of the sand, the windows fogged up and the music playing a slow, romantic song, and I couldn't think of one place else I'd rather be.

My hand drifted lazily beneath the sheets and circled around my aching cock. It was rock hard from the memories of the night before. I started to stroke myself, but one look at the clock and I knew I would have to wait. I'd lain there longer than I'd realized and if I didn't get a move on, I'd be late for my brunch with Gayle.

I made my way to the bathroom, being careful not to trip over the stack of boxes I'd left lying in the hallway, just waiting to be unpacked. I'd moved out of the house the week before, as soon as I'd found a decent condo to rent. It wasn't much, just a single bedroom, kitchen, and bath and a great view of the parking lot. But it was fairly new, didn't cost me an arm and a leg and was closer to work which shortened my commute.

I just had to keep reminding myself that it was only temporary. Once everything was settled in the divorce then I could start looking for something more permanent, something more my style. Perhaps something right along the beach with a big deck that I could sit on in the evenings and watch the sun setting out over the horizon.

I could picture Brooklyn spending a few weeks out of the summer there, telling me all about her day on the beach as I cooked hamburgers and hot dogs on the grill. I'd listen attentively to her and then smile as the door opened and Oliver walked out, carrying a cold salad of some kind.

My mind halted as I realized the direction of my thoughts and I chastised myself for getting carried away. Just because Oliver and I had shared a few incredible nights together and he'd basically sucked my brain through my dick the night before, didn't mean that either one of us were ready for a committed relationship. Hell, I had no idea if he was even looking for that at all. I mean, the first night we met, I watched him being fucked by another man. Of course, I was fucking a woman at the same time, so I had no right to judge. Still, I wondered if Oliver had given any thought to what he wanted or the direction we were headed.

I, on the other hand, had given it a lot of thought. I liked Oliver, plain and simple. I liked everything about him and the more time I spent with him, the more I began to care about him. He was so much more than a beautiful face with a killer body. He was quick witted, strong-willed and highly intelligent. His views on politics and religion as well as world events had led to some long and interesting conversations and I'd felt increasingly impressed by him with each one.

If it were up to me, I'd spend all my time with him. But it wasn't just up to me, Oliver had a say in things too. Not to mention the two women in my life who still had no clue that I was even involved with a man. Brooklyn would have to wait a bit longer, but I'd already decided that I was going to tell Gayle over brunch.

I just needed to finish working up my nerve. It wasn't that I was worried she'd respond badly, but it still would have to come as quite a shock to find out the man she'd been married to for eighteen years had been hiding such a huge part of himself. Guilt mixed in with my nerves and I hurried through my shower, eager to get the telling over with.

"Why did you knock?" Gayle asked with a laugh as she pulled the door open wide enough for me to walk past.

I shrugged my shoulders. "It didn't feel right to just walk in anymore. This is your house now."

Her eyes gentled as she laid a hand on my arm. "The fact that you're not living here doesn't make it any less your house. It belongs to both of us. Besides, I've already given it some thought, and I think after the divorce is final, maybe we could sell this place. I'd like to find something new, get a fresh start."

I smiled. As usual, we were in complete agreement. Was it any wonder we had worked so well together for so many years? "That sounds good to me."

Gayle let out a breath as if she'd been nervous about my response. I followed her into the kitchen where she already had fresh fruit and homemade cinnamon rolls on the table. She set to work scrambling some eggs while I poured us each a glass of orange juice.

The under-cabinet television that I'd bought her three Christmases ago was turned on to a home improvement show. Gayle never could stand for things to be too quiet, always wanting some form of background noise. I was sure being in that big house all by herself would've driven her crazy if she couldn't have either the TV or radio playing.

As I carried the glasses over to the table, the local station cut in with a breaking news alert and Gayle and I both turned to watch.

Another body had been discovered that morning in an alley behind a strip mall. Like the others, the young man was in his early twenties, thin, and good-looking with blond hair. He appeared to have been strangled to death.

"Jesus. That's the third one," Gayle whispered. I glanced over at her, but then directed my attention back to the TV.

They cut to where a spokesperson from the police department stood in front of a podium, looking haggard and stressed as several journalists vied for his attention. I wondered idly if that was his usual look or if he was just succumbing to the mounting stress of his job. A few seconds later, I could understand why he would as he went on to explain the similarities in each case and that they had enough evidence to believe that they were dealing with a serial killer.

A cold chill swept down my spine as he went on to warn all young men between the ages of eighteen and twenty-five to be cautious, avoid traveling anywhere alone after dark and to always be aware of their surroundings. My thoughts immediately flew to Oliver and the way he'd looked at me last night, so trusting and warm. I clamped down on those thoughts immediately, the possibility of anyone hurting him too painful to even think about.

A criminal psychologist was brought in to discuss the psychology behind strangulation murders. She explained that as a general rule, strangulation was a very personal way of murdering someone and oftentimes the murderer wound up being someone the victim knew intimately. She began discussing how strangulation differed from other murders such as a shooting, because strangling someone required the killer to be up close, often looking straight in their victim's eyes as the life bled out of them.

Another chill swept through my body and I was glad when Gayle switched the TV off. Still, I vowed to contact Oliver as soon as I was finished there so I could make sure he was aware of the danger within our city. Not that crime wasn't always a worry, but this particular person seemed to take a liking to men the same age and build as Oliver.

Gayle brought over a bowl of fresh, hot eggs and we settled in at the table. We made small talk as we ate, discussing work and how Brooklyn sounded the last time we'd each talked with her.

"So, I've met someone," we both said at the same time. We stared at each other with wide eyes for a second or two and then we burst out in a fit of laughter.

"Come on, I want all the details. What's her name? What's she like?" Gayle asked, resting her chin in her hands and staring at me excitedly.

"No. You first," I insisted, feeling like a bit of a coward.

"Okay," she said, laying her hands flat on the table and taking a deep breath. "His name is Andrew and we met at the second swap party. He was there alone, and we got to talking. He's an architect and widower. His wife passed away four years ago, and he'd tried all the dating apps and going to singles meet and greets. Finally, a friend invited him to a swap party and that's where we met."

Her smile had grown as she spoke about him and her eyes had a light shining in them that I wasn't sure I'd ever seen before. If I wasn't mistaken, I'd say she was falling for him hard, if she hadn't already.

"Does he have any children?"

Gayle shook her head. "No. He and his wife weren't able to have any, but I've told him all about Brooklyn and he's eager to meet her."

"He sounds wonderful. I'd love to meet him sometime, when you're ready," I said.

"Really?"

"Of course. You've got incredible instincts. Besides, anyone who can put that look on your face must be pretty special."

"Well, it's still really early. We agreed to take our time getting to know each other."

"I'm happy for you," I said honestly.

Gayle's smile grew watery. "Thank you, Sam. That's important to me. *You're* important to me."

I pulled her in for a hug and kissed her cheek. "I know and you're just as important to me. That'll never change," I promised.

Gayle wiped at her eyes and shook her head. "Sorry, I guess I was more worried about telling you than I realized."

"Believe me, I get it," I told her. Never one to miss anything, she tilted her head at me and narrowed her eyes.

"You seem a little on edge. What's going on?"

I ran my fingers through my hair, trying to figure out where to begin. One of the things I'd always liked about Gayle was that she never pushed. She'd ask a question and then wait patiently until I was ready to answer. I'd never appreciated that trait more than I did right then. Taking a deep breath, I decided to just dive right in.

"So, like I said, I've met someone. We met at the first party and it's just grown from there. We've had dinner together a few times and spent a lot of time talking on the phone and texting. Like you and Andrew, it's still pretty early, but I really like...him."

I stared down at my hands twisted in my lap, unable to meet her gaze. It was completely silent for all of two heartbeats and then Gayle spoke gently. "What's his name? Tell me everything."

I looked back up at her, blinking quickly as my eyes suddenly began to fill with tears. Until that moment, I hadn't given much thought to just how important her reaction would be to me. How could it not? Gayle had been my best friend, my confidant, and my rock for almost twenty years. Nearly half my life. Even when our families turned their backs on us, we'd stood by each other's sides, never faltering from what we believed was the right thing to do. Of course, her acceptance would be important to me. Not only her acceptance of me as a bisexual man, but of any future relationships I may have.

We continued talking for another hour or two. Gayle asked

questions and I answered them as openly and honestly as I could. I told her all about Oliver, although I left out some of the juicer bits. She seemed impressed that he was a model but was more interested in how he treated me and the way he made me feel, some of which I didn't have words for yet.

As we cleaned up the kitchen and loaded the dishwasher, we talked about how and where we would tell Brooklyn what was going on. Neither one of us were looking forward to that conversation, but she was coming home for a visit the following weekend. We knew we wouldn't be able to hide the fact that I was no longer living there, nor did we want to. We were both eager to start the next chapter of our lives.

In the end, we decided to treat this like we had everything else from the moment we found out she'd been conceived. We'd do it together and with as much kindness and compassion as possible.

ELEVEN

Oliver

Pulling up to the curb, I climbed tiredly out of my car and walked into the coffee shop. The delicious smell of fresh donuts and coffee hit me as soon as I stepped inside. Getting in line behind a mother and her two young kids, I did my best to ignore the tempting pastries lined up inside the glass counter.

I had plenty of time, but Korey had already started calling as soon as my alarm went off, wanting to know what time I planned on getting to the studio. Why he wanted me there at six thirty in the morning when he knew the photo shoot wasn't even scheduled until nine was beyond me. Hair and makeup only took an hour and then another half hour was spent with wardrobe checking for any last-minute adjustments that needed to be made. That still left me an hour to sit around and do what? Stare at the walls? No, thank you. I'd rather get a little more sleep instead.

Korey had always been a bit high-strung, but lately he'd become almost obsessive about my schedule. I'd been working no less than sixty hours a week each week for over a month and it was starting to take its toll. If I hadn't held my ground about having a couple of weekends off, I'm sure that number would've only increased.

And now, with him riding my ass about getting to the studio early, it was clear that we needed to have another talk. I worked hard, and I did my best with each and every job, but that didn't mean I wasn't allowed to have a life too. Especially now that I'd met someone I wanted to spend time with.

Just thinking about Samuel brought a smile to my face. I knew he'd had brunch with Gayle the day before. He'd told me he was planning on telling her then that he was bisexual, and my stomach had been in knots all morning, hoping it went well and that Samuel wouldn't get hurt.

He'd called that afternoon to tell me he'd gotten called into work with some emergency involving an ad campaign. While I understood his need to cancel our dinner date, I was disappointed not to be able to hear everything that had happened with Gayle. I ended up going for a run and then curling up in bed with some sushi and a Molly Ringwald movie marathon. Sometime around two in the morning, a text came through. I'd sat up in bed when I saw it was from Samuel.

Samuel: *I know you're probably sleeping. If so, I hope this doesn't wake you and you can read it in the morning. I just wanted to tell you how much I hated having to cancel our date. I always look forward to my time with you and not only because of the incredible things you can do with your mouth, although, that is a bonus. Haha. You're different from anyone I've ever met and when I'm with you…and now I'm starting to ramble. I'd apologize, but I think I'll just blame it on the fact that it's late and I'm exhausted. I'm going to get some sleep now, but there's a lot I need to talk to you about. Any chance we can have a redo on our date? No need to answer right away, I know you're probably asleep. I hope you're sleeping. Yes, totally rambling. I'm going now. Sweet dreams, Oliver.*

I'd fallen back against my pillows, clutching my phone to my chest and sporting the goofiest grin. Samuel was quite possibly the best mix of sexy and adorable that I'd ever met. I shot back a quick response.

Me: *I'd love a redo. How about dinner and a movie at my place after work? Oh, and just so you know… I haven't even begun to show you what I can do with my mouth.*

He'd sent back a line of drooling emojis and I'd fallen asleep with a smile on my face. Samuel was different from anyone else I'd met too…in all the best ways.

When it was finally my turn at the counter, I ordered a large coffee with cream and sugar for myself and black coffees for everyone else. That way they could doctor them up however they liked. And if I was lucky, showing up with coffee would help improve Korey's mood as well.

I slid over in front of the cash register while the barista set to work filling my order. The girl behind the register couldn't have been any older than seventeen and I knew the minute she recognized me because her eyes doubled in size.

"Hey! How are you?" I asked.

"I'm…I'm good," she said, stumbling over her words. She reached up and tucked her blonde hair behind her ear.

"Order for Oliver," the barista said as she set my tray of coffees down on the counter.

"I knew it! You're Oliver Hughes, aren't you?" the cashier exclaimed loudly. A few heads turned to stare, but I just smiled back at her.

"Yes, I am. It's nice to meet you…Shelly," I said, reading the nametag on her shirt. Her eyes lit up and she giggled, smoothing the hair behind her ear once again in what must have been a nervous habit of hers.

"You too," she giggled again.

"Shelly, hurry up!" the barista scolded.

"Oh, sorry," she said as if she'd forgotten she was supposed to be working. "Let me just ring you up."

"Thank you," I said, reaching into my back pocket for my wallet. Shelly read me the total and I handed her my card. A few seconds later, her brow furrowed.

"Um, it says it's declined," she whispered over the counter.

"That's not possible. Would you mind trying again, please?" I asked politely.

"Oh, of course." I watched as she ran it through again, but I could tell it hadn't worked that time either when her brows scrunched up.

"I'm really sorry, Oliver. It still says it's declined." She handed it back to me with an apologetic look on her face.

"No, it's not your fault," I said absently as I stuffed the card back in my wallet and pulled out a different one. "Here, this one should do it." I held my breath as she swiped the card then breathed a sigh of relief moments later when she smiled and handed it back to me, along with a copy of the receipt to sign.

"That kind of thing happens all the time. I'm sure it was just our machine or maybe some mix-up on the card company's end. Just give them a call and I'm sure they'll get everything sorted out," Shelly suggested, clearly relieved to see everything work out.

"I'm sure. Thank you very much," I told her as I handed her back the receipt.

I shoved my wallet back in my pocket and then grabbed my drinks and headed out the door. I set them carefully in the passenger seat and then went around and climbed behind the wheel. My hands were shaking as I took hold of the steering wheel and one look in the rearview mirror showed that my face was bright red. I'd never been more embarrassed in my life, and on top of that, I was confused.

I had no idea how that could've happened or what went wrong, but I was going to have to talk to Korey if I wanted to find out.

When I'd first signed him on as my agent, he'd suggested getting both of our names put on the business bank account and credit cards. He'd told me that if his name was on them then he could keep track of things and pay the balance each month, leaving me free to focus on my work. And it had worked well for us...until a few moments before.

I sighed. Maybe Shelly was right, and it was just some glitch with their machine or the credit card company's system. Or maybe Korey was more stressed than I'd realized, and he was starting to let things slip through the cracks.

A wave of guilt washed over me. I should be taking a more active role in those things instead of leaving it all on Korey's shoulders. It wasn't fair to him and was probably the reason he'd been so crabby lately. Determined to sort things out with him, I started the car and merged into traffic.

Korey was on a business call when I got there and then I was whisked away to get my hair and makeup done. I watched him slip out the door just before we broke for lunch and he didn't return until the end of my shoot. It was getting late then, and I just wanted to get home, take a shower, and curl up on the couch with Samuel, but I knew I needed to talk with Korey first.

"Hey! I just saw some of the photos from today and you looked great," he said as I was shoving my things in my bag.

I grinned at him over my shoulder "Thanks. Greg has a great eye for detail and he knows exactly what he wants from each shot. I like working with him."

"Good. Maybe we can pair the two of you up on some future projects. It's been a long day though and I don't feel like cooking. You want to grab a bite to eat before you go home?"

"Sorry, I can't. I have plans already," I told him. I finished shoving everything in my bag then swung it over my shoulder and turned so I could face him.

Korey narrowed his eyes at me. "You have plans? Is it that same guy you've been mooning over for the last few weeks?"

I frowned. "I've told you his name several times already. It's Samuel and if you must know, yes, he's who I have plans with."

"Whoa!" he said, holding his hands up. "I didn't mean anything by it. It's just, you've been spending a lot of time with him lately. What all do you know about this guy?"

I clenched my jaw, trying to rein in my temper. I knew Korey was only concerned about me because he was my friend. "I know enough to tell that he's a really great guy and he wouldn't do anything to hurt me."

"Fine. I hope you're right." I cocked my head at him. "What? I'm being serious. You can never be too careful, Oliver. There are a lot of crazies out there."

"Yeah, well you would know," I deadpanned. He looked startled at first, but then he laughed as I lost the ability to hide my smirk.

"Whatever. All I'm saying is you should really get to know this guy before you let him get too close."

"Yes, Dad," I responded, rolling my eyes.

Korey let out a long-suffering sigh but walked me out to my car. I debated whether to bring the credit card issue up right then, but it had been so long since I'd seen him being anything but completely uptight and I didn't really want to rock the boat. Maybe I'd just look into things myself. That way he wouldn't have to worry about it. Especially if it ended up being something as simple as a computer error. We said goodnight and I climbed in my car. My phone rang just then, and I hurried to answer when I saw it was Samuel.

"You better not be calling to cancel," I joked.

"Not on your life," he responded. The deep timber of his voice sent a delicious shiver down my spine. "Are you done working for the day?"

"Yes, thankfully," I sighed.

"Uh oh. Bad day, baby?" My breath caught as I wondered if he'd meant to call me that, but then warmth bloomed inside my chest when he made no apologies or excuses.

"Umm, it wasn't bad so much as it was a long day."

"Well, you go on home and take a hot shower to relax yourself. I'll pick up some dinner for us and head on over."

"Has anyone ever told you that you're a prince?" I said teasingly.

"A god, yes, but a prince, no," he joked back. I laughed, loving the back and forth between us. This was just what I needed after a long, tiring day.

"Well, I'm telling you, you're a prince. We'll need to do a little more exploring before I'll know if you've reached god status or not."

"Oh, I do love a challenge."

We hung up and I hurried home and jumped in the shower. I had just finished pulling on some clothes when the doorbell rang. I looked in the mirror and ran my fingers through my still-damp hair. I wished I'd had time to do something with it before he got there. I hadn't even had time to apply any makeup.

I shrugged at my reflection. I suppose he was bound to see me that way eventually. At least if everything kept going as I hoped. I rushed out to the living room and pulled the door open. Samuel was standing there, balancing three white paper bags in his arms and wearing a broad grin.

"I got Chinese. Only I wasn't sure what you liked so I ordered a variety to choose from," he said.

I chuckled as I grabbed a bag from him and led him into the kitchen. "Are you sure you just got a variety and not one of everything off the menu?" I joked. I had just set my bag down when a strong set of arms slid around my waist.

"I would've bought the whole damn restaurant if I thought it would make you happy," he whispered as he began trailing a line of kisses up the side of my neck. I tilted my head to give him better access.

"I don't need a restaurant," I said, moaning as he bit down on the lobe of my ear.

"You don't?"

"Nope," I said, turning in his arms and running my hands up into his hair. "You make me happy all on your own."

My tongue darted out to lick my lips and then his mouth was on mine and I was lost to everything but the taste of his lips and the feel of his hands running up and down my spine. I wasn't sure how long we stayed that way, but we were both panting by the time we pulled away and I was very pleased to see I wasn't the only one who had to adjust himself.

I grabbed a couple of plates and we took turns scooping out the food we wanted from the various cartons then we headed to the living room. We sat, facing each other on the couch and over dinner, took turns talking about our day. Samuel told me everything that had happened with Gayle and how well she'd taken the news.

"She sounds like such an incredible person," I told him.

"She is. I'm very lucky that we've been able to stay friends through all of this and that she's been so supportive."

"Well, I think she could say the same about you." Samuel stared down at his plate, but I could see the small smile on his lips.

"Anyway, I just have to get through next weekend. Brooklyn's coming home for a visit and we decided that we needed to go ahead and tell her what's going on." He set his plate down on the coffee table and leaned back. I could see the tightness around the corners of his eyes and the concern hidden in their blue depths. I didn't like seeing him worry.

I set my own plate aside and crawled onto his lap. His arms came around me automatically and I cupped his face. "From everything you've told me, Brooklyn's a smart and compassionate girl.

A trait she inherited from both of her parents. She may be upset at first, but you won't lose her."

"You think so?" Samuel asked quietly.

"I do. And if you need to talk afterward, just call me. Or come over. I'm sure I can think of ways to relieve your stress," I said, wagging my brows up and down. Samuel let out a low chuckle and then he lowered me onto the couch and we spent the next few hours making out like a couple of teenagers.

TWELVE

Samuel

looked up at Gayle in surprise as her hand landed on my leg. "If you don't stop bouncing so much, security is going to think you're up to no good," she teased.

I blew out a breath. "I can't help it. I couldn't sleep at all last night, worrying about what was going to happen when we tell Brooklyn. I keep going back and forth between wanting to get it over with and wishing we never had to tell her at all. Now her flight is delayed, and I'm about to lose my goddamn mind. And how the hell are you staying so calm?" I demanded.

Gayle chuckled. "Oh, I'm not calm. Far from it, in fact, but I took two Valiums before leaving the house." I stared at her, trying to see if she was serious. Gayle had always been strongly opposed to taking medicine. She rarely even took over-the-counter stuff, claiming she didn't like the way they made her feel. Two Valiums should have knocked her on her butt, but she just looked mellow instead.

"Well, okay. Next time would you mind sharing though?" I joked.

She laughed at that. "Next time? How many times do you plan on getting divorced?" I laughed too then, and my shoulders began to loosen up. Until I checked the list of flights on the monitor and saw that Brooklyn's flight had just arrived and then my stomach plummeted, and my nerves came back with a vengeance. Gayle grabbed my hand and squeezed it and her mouth settled into a thin line.

"It's going to be okay. We raised a smart and compassionate daughter. She'll be upset at first, but we're not going to lose her," I said, repeating what Oliver had said to me. Somehow, just saying those words brought a level of comfort to me.

I spotted Brooklyn as she walked toward the baggage claim area and my heart went straight to my throat. In the back of my mind, I'd been worried that she'd change too much once she was gone, but she was still the same beautiful young woman she was a few months ago when she'd said goodbye.

Her eyes lit up as soon as she saw us, and she came running toward us with her arm wide open. "Mommy! Daddy!" She screeched as she dove into our arms. The three of us stood there, hugging and crying and then laughing at ourselves because we were crying.

I bent my head and breathed in the familiar scent of her strawberry shampoo, savoring the moment. I'd been so caught up worrying about everything that could go wrong, that I forgot about the one thing that would be perfectly right. My baby girl was home.

Brooklyn climbed in the back seat and chattered the whole way home about her new school, which classes she loved as well as which ones she hated and about her new friends. She told us how disgusting the cafeteria food was and about how her roommate refused to clean up after herself, but that they loved each other anyway. I'd forgotten how vivacious our daughter could be.

Gayle and I hadn't had the chance to say more than two words since we got in the car, but neither of us were complaining. For now, we were just content listening to our daughter and seeing how happy she was. We exchanged looks across the front seat and even though she was smiling, I knew Gayle was having the same thoughts I was. What would our news do to our daughter? Would she ever be this carefree again? I took Gayle's hand and gave it a gentle squeeze then I forced my thoughts aside and focused on Brooklyn as she described a project that she was working on for one of her classes.

I carried Brooklyn's suitcase upstairs and laid it down on her bed then I went back down to the kitchen where the two women were busy getting dinner ready. Gayle had left her special homemade spaghetti sauce cooking in the crockpot all day and had pasta boiling in a pot on the stove. Brooklyn set the table while I put together a salad and soon we were sitting down to eat.

We were halfway through our meal when Brooklyn looked at each of us. "So, I've told you all about me. What's new with you guys?"

I froze with my fork halfway to my mouth and Gayle shot me a panicky look. I set my fork down and took a drink of water, carefully trying to decide what to say first. Brooklyn's eyes darted back and forth between us as she picked up on the tension in the room. I reached for her hand and cupped it in my own. "Sweetheart, your mom and I have something to talk to you about."

"What's going on?" she asked.

I squeezed her fingers and Gayle reached for her other hand. "After you left for school, your dad and I had a long talk. You know that we love you very much and we love each other too, right?" She waited until Brooklyn nodded. "Well, the thing is, we realized that while we love each other, we're not *in love* with each other anymore."

"What?" Brooklyn gasped, darting her eyes to each of our faces.

"What your mom's saying is, we realized that we're better as friends than a couple," I added.

"So, what does this mean? Are you getting a divorce?" Brooklyn's voice sounded small and scared and I felt part of my heart breaking.

Gayle and I looked at each other and then we nodded. "We still love each other, and we talk all the time, probably more than we did before because now we're able to be completely honest about how we're feeling. In a way, this has brought us closer together."

"I don't get it. If you're talking and even closer and you both still love each other, then why are you splitting up? Why not go to marriage counseling or try going on some dates to bring the spark back?" Brooklyn asked, her voice rising as she became more upset.

"Honey, it doesn't work that way," Gayle started, but Brooklyn cut her off.

"Then how *does* it work, Mom? Because I thought when you loved someone you did whatever it took to stay together." The two of them stared at each other and I could see that neither knew quite what to say next.

"Do you remember us telling you how your mom and I met?" I jumped in.

Brooklyn turned to me. "You were both in college, right?"

"Right. We were not much older than you. It was our freshman year and we met at a party. Things got a little out of hand and the next thing we knew, you were on the way. We got married soon after and then you were born, and we were so elated to have you. Don't ever doubt how much we wanted you," I told her, looking right into her eyes to be sure she heard me.

"But my point is, we barely knew each other when we decided to get married. We were scared to death back then and had no idea what we were doing. It forged an unbreakable bond between us which developed into a strong friendship. Eventually, that friendship turned into a deep mutual respect and even love, but we never were in love with each other," I explained.

"So, both of you are okay with this?" She looked at us like she still wasn't quite sure.

"We really are, honey," Gayle assured her. "I want your father to be happy and he wants the same for me. We're both fully supportive of each other." She glanced at me as she said it.

"What? Is there something else I need to know?" Brooklyn asked almost hysterically.

I took a deep breath. "There is something else. Your mother knows now, but it's something that I wasn't even sure about myself until recently."

Brooklyn pulled her hands away from each of us and folded them across her chest. "What?" she asked flatly.

I clasped my hands in my lap to try and keep them from shaking, but I realized that it wasn't just my hands; tremors had begun to rock my whole body. I don't think I'd ever been more afraid of anything in my entire life. The look in her eyes told me that she had already guessed what it was, but I still owed it to her and to myself to say the words.

"I'm bisexual."

Brooklyn's chair scraped across the tile floor as she pushed away from the table and stood. "I can't...I don't...I can't be here right now. I'll be at Jenny's if there's an emergency." With that, she grabbed her car keys off the hook by the door and headed out.

I stood, ready to go after her, but Gayle stopped me by grabbing my arm. "Let her go for now." I whipped my head in her direction, angry that she didn't want to chase after our daughter just as much as I did.

"She needs some time," she said softly. "We threw an awful lot at her at once. Give her some time to absorb it all. She'll be safe over at Jenny's and we can try and talk to her again tomorrow."

I felt myself deflate, the anger rushing out of me as quickly as it had set in. I knew Gayle was right and that if I pushed Brooklyn right then, I could wind up doing even more damage. But God, did it hurt. Pain wracked my being because I'd just hurt the most important person in my life and there wasn't a damn thing I could do about it.

"Do you need me to stay?" I asked quietly.

She shook her head sadly. "No, I think I'll leave this here until morning and go soak in a hot bath for a while."

"Okay. Call me if you need anything." We hugged each other, and I kissed her on the forehead then let myself out.

I drove around aimlessly for a while. My head was spinning with all the what-ifs. What if Brooklyn can't forgive me? What if she feels so betrayed that she never wants to come home again? What if she never trusts me again? What if I'd just lost her for good?

She'd been hurt and confused by the news of Gayle's and my split. Any kid would be when they found out their parents were getting a divorce, but she seemed like she was trying to make sense of it. I could see her working it out in her head and I had faith that she'd come around, eventually. Then I dropped my bombshell, and everything changed. I could see her shutting down and putting up walls to protect herself. It was all there on her face, as clear as day, and it felt like someone had stabbed me in the chest.

Brooklyn had always been close to both me and Gayle, but there was a special bond between me and my daughter that was unique to only the two of us. When she was little, she was my constant shadow; helping me fix things around the house and pitching in as I made breakfast on Saturday mornings. Even as a teenager, when most parents had to force their kids to spend time with them, she would be right by my side, helping me do yardwork, or curled up on the couch with a book while I watched TV.

There'd always been a look in her eyes that let me know that she trusted me to keep her safe. That look had said that she knew I'd always be there for her without fail, and that I would never, ever cause her pain. But I had hurt her. Badly. And the trust in her eyes had been replaced with utter devastation and betrayal. I tried to push the vision away, but my mind betrayed me, insistently playing it over and over again on an endlessly painful loop.

My body was still trembling, full of emotions that I had no idea what to do with. I was barely holding on and I knew it wasn't safe for me to be driving. I considered going back to my condo, but the last thing I wanted was to be in that cold and unfamiliar place, surrounded by boxes of memories of a family that had been torn apart. I didn't want to be alone. I needed someone to hold me together while I fell apart.

I needed Oliver.

It didn't take me long to get to his place and then I was standing in front of his door. My hand was shaking as I lifted it in the air to knock and a strong tremor rocked my body as everything I'd been holding in threatened to spill out. I knocked on his door, and it was only a few seconds before he opened it. He took one look at my face and opened his arms wide for me.

I collapsed into his embrace right as the dam burst and a torrent of tears broke free. Oliver never let go, but somehow, he managed to get both of us inside and shut the door. His arms wrapped around me and he held me so tightly that I could feel his heart beating against my own chest. I buried my face in the crook of his neck and I knew I had to be soaking his shirt, but he never once complained. Instead, he began to sway, gently rocking me back and forth while I cried.

Once in a while he would kiss the side of my head or whisper in my ear that he was there and that I wasn't alone, but mostly, he just held me. He was sweet, and he was loving, and I was so thankful to have him because he was absolutely everything I needed.

When the worst of the sobbing had passed, he led me over to the couch and we sat down. He never interrupted as I told him everything that had happened; from picking Brooklyn up at the airport and how thrilled she was with her new life to the difficult conversation that led to that final, devastated look on her face.

"And now, I don't know," I said with a shrug. "She was so upset. I don't know if I can make her understand or if she'll even be willing to listen to me at all. I may have lost her for good," I finished saying and then drew in a ragged breath. I had no idea how it was possible to have any tears left, but my eyes began to fill up anyhow.

Oliver's eyes were full of compassion as he cupped my face and used his thumbs to wipe the tears from my cheeks. Speaking softly, he said, "I don't know Brooklyn personally, so I can't really say for sure what she'll do. But what I do know is that she was raised by a mother who is strong and supportive and refreshingly non-judgmental, based on how she's treated you.

"She also has a father who is kind and caring and who never even bats an eye when the guy he's dating wears makeup or high heels. A man who looked beyond the face of a model, which is all most people see, and took the time to get to know the person underneath. You and Gayle both obviously look beyond the superficial and you have raised your daughter to do the same. You've raised her to find the truth in a person's actions instead of just what they say."

I leaned my cheek into his hand, letting his warmth soak into my skin as I listened to his words and felt my first spark of hope. "She's hurting right now, and she probably feels like her foundation has been rocked a bit, but I honestly believe that after some time, she'll want to talk. And when she does, you can remind her that even though your life is changing, you're still her father and your love for her is still as strong as it's ever been."

"How did you get so wise?" I gave him a watery smile.

Oliver's smile was surer. "I just listen and watch, and I think I've gotten to know you pretty well. You are a good man, Samuel Bishop. You changed your entire life to do right by that little girl and she has that same goodness in her. She won't turn her back on you, I'm sure of it."

"Oliver?"

"Yes?"

"I'm so tired."

"I know, honey."

"Oliver?"

"Yes?"

"I don't want to be alone tonight."

Without another word, he took my hand and led me down the hallway and into his room. There was nothing sexual in his movements as he began undressing me. I'd had a whirlwind of emotions go through my body that day and it was as if he could sense, without me having to say anything, that anymore might break me.

Instead, he stripped me down to my underwear then held the sheets back, so I could climb into bed. My eyes grew heavy as he removed his own clothes and then climbed into bed next to me. I reached for him and he slid his arms around me as I laid my head on his chest. The feel of his fingers running through my hair and the sound of his heart beating beneath my ear pulled me further down until I finally drifted off to sleep.

THIRTEEN

Samuel

My eyes felt swollen and gritty as I opened them and peeked out at the morning. I'd barely slept the night before, tossing and turning, plagued by bad dreams that would jolt me awake, only to pull me back under when I remembered that they were real. I felt bad waking Oliver with my restlessness, but he never complained, he just wrapped his arms around me and would rub his fingers up and down my back in soothing patterns until I started to doze again.

I took the time to stare at him, drinking him in and reveling in how gorgeous he looked first thing in the morning. He lay facing me on the bed, still sound asleep; his hair all mussed, lines on his cheek from being pressed against his pillow and his long lashes fanning over his cheeks. Even without a stitch of makeup on or his hair professionally styled, he was the most exquisite-looking man I'd ever seen.

My phone chirped from somewhere in the room. Trying not to wake him, I rolled over and climbed out of bed. Sometime in the night, Oliver must have gotten up and folded my clothes for me. He'd even found an extra charger and put my phone on it. I looked over my shoulder at his sleeping form and my heart swelled with emotions. I had no idea what I could've done in my life to be lucky enough to find a man as thoughtful as Oliver, but now that I had, I never wanted to let him go. We needed to talk, and soon. I needed to know if he felt for me even half the things that I was feeling for him. But that would have to wait for another time.

I pulled my phone off the charger, sure the text was going to be from Gayle. Knowing her, she would've been up bright and early, formulating a plan for getting our daughter to listen. So, I was shocked when the name on the screen popped up as My Girl, the name I'd assigned to Brooklyn's contact information.

My Girl: *I'd like to talk.*

My heart pounded wildly against my ribs as I read over her words and then I read them again, just to be sure. She wanted to talk. My hands were shaking as I typed out a reply.

Me: *I'd love to. When and where?*
My Girl: *Ellington Park in an hour? I'll meet you by the playground.*
Me: *I'll be there. And thank you. I love you.*

She sent a single red heart back. It wasn't much, but at least she hadn't just ignored my "I love you." Checking the time, I quickly pulled on my clothes and shoes then crept over to the bed and knelt down beside it. Oliver had rolled over but was still sound asleep. That's what happens when you keep him awake all night with your tossing and turning, I thought guiltily. I hated to wake him up now that he was finally getting some rest, but I also didn't want to leave without saying goodbye. I reached over and brushed his bangs out of his face. His lashes fluttered as his eyes drifted open and he gave me a warm, sleep-softened smile.

"You okay?" he whispered, stretching his hand out from under the covers to cup my cheek. I circled my hand around his wrist and turned my face into his hand, so I could place a kiss in the center of his palm.

"I'm fine, thanks to you. I'm sorry to wake you, but I need to go. Brooklyn texted me and she wants to talk."

"She does?" he asked, both his eyes and his smile widening.

"Yeah. So, I need to get going. I don't want to be late."

"Of course. Go! Call me later and let me know how it goes, okay? Or…you could stop by if you want to. I have a few errands to run but other than that, I'll be here," he said sweetly.

"Thank you. And thank you for last night. I don't know what I would've done without you." I leaned down and kissed him, letting my lips convey everything I was feeling. When I pulled back, Oliver's eyes were unfocused, and he was breathing a little heavier than before.

"Try and get some more sleep," I whispered, but his eyes were already starting to drift shut again. Smiling, I stood up and left the room. I turned the lock on his front door knob and then pulled it closed behind me.

I raced home and took a quick shower, brushed my teeth, and put on a clean outfit before heading back out to my car. Somehow, I doubted it would help the situation with my daughter for me to show up in the same clothes as the night before, regardless of the fact that nothing had happened.

As I drove to the park, I wondered what would happen once I saw Brooklyn. She'd said she wanted to talk, not that she was willing to listen. Maybe she'd just asked me there, so she could tell me that she no longer wanted me to be a part of her life. My chest tightened as I even considered that scenario. I'd like to think that it wasn't a possibility, but at that point, I really wasn't sure.

I think that was one of the hardest things for me about the entire situation. The distance between me and Brooklyn. She'd always wanted to spend time with me while she was growing up, but there had also never been anything we couldn't say to each other. She'd always been able to talk to me about a boy at school who liked her or if her feelings had been bruised by one of her friends. Most of the time I could read her moods or tell what she was thinking just by looking at her, but if someone asked me right then what the outcome of this meeting would be, I'd have to answer with an "I don't know."

I pulled onto park property and slowed the car to the required ten miles per hour. It was a beautiful morning and the sun was shining. People were out taking advantage of the nice weather, but I didn't pay them any attention as I pulled into a spot near the playground and searched the area for my daughter. After a few seconds, I spotted her. She was standing with her arms wrapped around herself, staring at a group of children who were busy playing in a sandbox.

I reached into the back seat and grabbed the jacket I'd brought with me in case I got cold then I climbed out of the car. She turned as I approached and my heart ached at the puffy look to her eyes and the dark smudges on the delicate skin underneath. I gave her a small smile and held out the jacket.

"You looked like you might be cold," I said.

She stared at me for a second as if she were trying to figure something out then she stepped closer and slid her arms into the sleeves while I held it open for her. "Thank you," she murmured. She stepped away again and stared at the ground, like she wasn't sure what to do next.

"Would you like to take a walk around the lake?" I suggested.

She gave me a relieved look. "Yeah, okay." I followed her as we went around the children building sandcastles and a guy who was tossing a frisbee to his German Shepherd.

We were silent as we stepped onto the concrete path that circled the lake and slowly began making our way around. It wasn't exactly awkward between us, but it definitely wasn't as effortless as our time spent together usually was. I wanted to jump in, rattling off anything at all to get the ball rolling, but she was the one who had asked to meet, and I owed it to her to let her take her time and figure out what she wanted to say. We were about halfway around when she finally spoke.

"I'm sorry I ran out last night. I just needed some time to sort things out in my head."

"You don't need to apologize. I'm sure it all came as quite a shock."

She shoved her hands down into the pockets of my jacket. "There's so much I just don't get," she said, her face scrunching up.

"If you tell me which parts you don't understand, maybe I can help you make sense of it," I offered.

"All of it?" she responded, letting out a humorless laugh. "No, I think I understand about you and Mom not being in love, but was it always that way? Were you each just going through the motions all these years?"

"Yes and no," I told her. I went on to explain when she shot me a confused look. "Yes, it was always that way, in the sense that we've never been in love with each other, but no, we weren't just going through the motions all these years because neither one of us realized that we weren't in love. Neither of us had ever really dated much before each other so we had nothing to compare it to. The only thing we knew was that we were happy. Happy with each other and happy being your parents."

"So, what changed? What made you figure out you weren't in love?"

"I don't know that there was a definitive moment. I think the closer the time came for us to let you go, the more we started taking stock of our own lives. We started thinking about all the things we hadn't done yet and where we saw ourselves five, ten years from now and neither of us were able to see the other in that picture. At least not as anything more than close friends," I explained.

"So, if I'd stayed home, this might not have happened?" My head whipped toward her, shocked that she would even think such a thing and saw her eyes swimming with tears. I stopped walking and pulled her into my arms. If she wanted to push me away, I'd let her go, but I couldn't just stand there and see my daughter hurting without reaching out for her. She didn't hug me back, but she didn't push me away either.

"That is the farthest thing from the truth. You had nothing to do with our splitting up and even if you hadn't gone off to college, you would've left eventually anyway, and you were supposed to. It's our job as parents to raise you to be the best person you can be and then let you go out into the world, so you can make it a better place."

I heard her let out a ragged breath and I wondered how long she'd been holding that in. She pulled away from me and we resumed our walk until we came up to a bench. I motioned to it and she nodded so we both sat down, looking out over the water.

"It's going to take some time, but I think I'll be able to wrap my head around why you and Mom are getting divorced. The thing I'm having the most trouble with is the part about you being bisexual," she said flatly, and my heart sank to my stomach like a lead balloon.

"What do you mean? Does it bother you that I like men?" I asked softly. She turned to look at me and I held my breath as I waited for her answer. I didn't want to make things worse between us, but now that I'd figured that part of myself out, I couldn't just push it away as if it didn't exist. I wouldn't.

Her mouth dropped open. "Oh my God! No, of course not!" she exclaimed. "Dad, I've got lots of friends who are members of the LGBT community. In high school, I was part of the gay/straight alliance, remember?"

"Then I don't understand. Why is that the part that you're having the most trouble with?"

She sighed like the answer should be obvious. "I don't care that you like guys. I care that you lied to me about it. I thought we could talk about anything, and now I find out you've been keeping this massive secret from me. And I don't know if I'm more upset by the fact that I feel like I don't know you, or the thought of you feeling like you had to hide your entire life."

"Honey, you've got it wrong. It wasn't like that at all," I interjected.

"Then please, explain it to me." Her blue eyes were wide as she begged for me to make her understand.

I reached for her hand, thankful when she didn't pull away. "The first time I realized I might like guys was in eighth grade. I had this English teacher. Mr. Lasseter was his name and he had these eyes and this smile that just drew me in. Then, in high school, I'd catch myself checking out the other guys. I was confused and didn't really know what was going on because I still liked girls and thought they were pretty. But I noticed that while all my friends were talking about girls, none of them ever mentioned that hot new boy that had just moved to our town or the way the baseball coach's pants fit just perfectly when he bent down to tie his shoes."

Brooklyn gave me a small smile and squeezed my hand. "Back then, people didn't talk about being gay all that much and I'd never even heard of the word bisexual. It would've helped explain an awful lot if I had, but even if I'd known, I never would've been able to tell anybody in that little town. I wasn't even sure if I really liked guys or not. All I knew was that I wasn't quite the same as everyone else.

"I kept quiet all through high school, but I decided that once I got to college, I'd find out what was going on, one way or another. Before I ever got the chance though, I went to a party and met your mom and you know what happened from there." I held my hand up to stop her as she opened her mouth, already anticipating the conclusion she would've drawn from my story.

"No. Do not even think that it was your fault in any way, shape or form. Your mother and I made our own decisions that night and those decisions had consequences. Beautiful, wonderful consequences that I wouldn't trade for the world. I was telling you the truth when I said you were my biggest joy." Tears were streaming down her face at that point and I reached over to wipe them away.

"I never regretted my decision to marry your mom and raise you. I still don't. But it also meant that I had to put my own life aside and create a new one; one that included being a husband and a father. I was never miserable, and I never felt like I was hiding anything, because I wasn't even sure what I was really feeling to begin with. Plus, I still liked girls and your mom was quite the looker. Still is." Brooklyn gave me her first genuine grin when she heard that.

"So, I'm assuming something happened to make you sure. I mean, you seemed pretty sure when you told me."

My face colored a bit and her eyes grew wide. "Who is he? I want details. I mean, not *details*, details because ewww! But tell me!"

I couldn't help but smile at her excitement and I felt like a five-ton weight had been lifted off my chest. I took a deep breath, feeling my lungs fully expand for the first time since we'd left to go to the airport. It was in that moment that I knew we were going to be okay.

"His name is Oliver…"

FOURTEEN

Oliver

The plane was dark except for a few rows ahead where someone had switched on their reading light. I glanced over at Korey who was sound asleep in the seat next to me, having thankfully passed out after just two hours into the ten-and-a-half-hour flight to London. He'd been in such a terrible mood since he'd picked me up that I hadn't dared bring up the credit card issue. I hoped he didn't plan on behaving that way the entire trip or we may have to have a come-to-Jesus moment.

He'd rolled his shirtsleeves up before he fell asleep and I took a minute to look over the scratches along his wrist and arms. I'd noticed he had a couple on his cheek as well. When I'd asked him about them, he told me he'd lost the battle with a rosebush he was trimming at his mother's house. I wasn't sure which surprised me the most; that he'd been gardening, or the fact that he had a mother who lived nearby that I'd never met.

The scratches on his face weren't bad, but the ones along his arms were fairly deep in a few places. I'd have to make sure he put some antibiotic cream on them when we got to London, so they wouldn't get infected. With that plan in mind, I tried to settle in once more.

I'd tried reclining in my seat, a soft pillow under my head and a warm blanket over my lap, but still, I couldn't manage to fall asleep. It could've been the noise of the plane's engines or perhaps Korey's constant snoring that was keeping me awake, but I was pretty sure it had mostly to do with having to leave Samuel. As our relationship continued to grow and I began falling for him, I found myself resenting the times we had to spend apart more and more. Samuel understood that I had to travel for my job and, while he never made me feel bad for it, we both missed each other terribly, especially when it was for long periods of time.

Luckily, I was only going to be gone three days this trip and most of that would be spent flying back and forth. I would've bowed out of this one altogether, but I'd been asked to take part in a show for the new Armani collection and rumor had it that Kate Middleton herself was going to be there. I was pretty sure I would die if I ever got to meet her. As far as I was concerned, she was the best thing to happen to England since Diana, Princess of Wales.

I turned on my side and adjusted my pillow, so I wouldn't get a crick in my neck, then I closed my eyes and let my mind drift. The nameless, faceless man who used to star in all my dreams was nothing more than a memory now, replaced by someone with bright blue eyes, a killer body, and a smile that made my knees go weak. Samuel was every fantasy I'd ever had, come to life.

I felt myself smile as the memories of the night before washed over me. *Samuel and I hadn't seen each other since he'd left to meet with Brooklyn. I'd spent that day scrubbing my apartment until every single inch of it gleamed. I couldn't help it; whenever I got anxious, I channeled that energy into cleaning and I was more nervous that day than I could remember being in a very long time. I was dying to know how things were going and I'd nearly driven myself crazy, constantly checking my phone to be sure I hadn't missed a call or text from him. When my phone actually did ring, I almost had a heart attack.*

THE SWAP

Samuel had called to tell me that everything had gone well and that he'd tell me everything later, but Brooklyn had asked him to spend the day with her and Gayle before she had to go back to school. I was disappointed that I wouldn't get to see him before my trip, but I was also so relieved that everything seemed to be better between him and his daughter that I immediately got choked up. I was sure he could hear the wavering of my voice as I told him to have a wonderful time and that I'd see him when I got back.

I spent the rest of the afternoon packing for my trip and going over the itinerary. I considered going for a jog, but one look out the window showed me that it was starting to get dark and with a serial killer on the loose, I figured that might not be the best idea. Just the thought of those poor guys, fighting to survive as some sick bastard choked the life out of them, sent cold chills up my spine.

Deciding to stay in, I heated up some leftover minestrone soup and camped out on the couch in my favorite unicorn jammies, watching old black-and-white movies. I didn't care what the storylines were, I just liked seeing all the clothes and hairstyles back then. They may not have been very progressive in their thinking, but they sure dressed in style.

When I woke up, it was even darker out and there was a different movie on the TV. It took me a few seconds to figure out what had woken me, but then I heard it again, a gentle knock on the door. I grabbed my phone to check the time. Who the hell could be knocking on my door at ten o'clock at night? **I swear to God, if it's Korey, I'm going to kill him.**

I stumbled to the door, rubbing my hands over my eyes and releasing a tired yawn. One look through the peephole had my heart racing though and suddenly I was wide awake. I quickly ran my fingers through my hair, hoping it didn't look like a rat's nest and cupped my hand in front of my face, blowing into it to check my breath. I glanced down at my pajamas and cursed the fact that I wasn't in something sheer and silky instead. **Oh well. Nothing I can do about it now.**

I pulled the door open and started to say hello, but I never got the chance as Samuel rushed forward and grabbed me up in a kiss that left my head woozy and my toes curled. Oh. My. God. The man could kiss! With our tongues exploring and my fingers in his hair, his hands slid around my waist, pulling me up against him so I could feel exactly how excited he was to see me.

His hands slid down to cup my ass and lifted me easily into the air. I wrapped my legs around his waist, locking my ankles together to hold him in place and began thrusting my hips so that our cocks rubbed against each other. Samuel growled deep in his throat, then swallowed my gasp as the rough denim of his jeans pressed through the thin layer of cotton I had on.

"I didn't. Think I'd. Get to see you," I managed to say in between kisses.

"Had to. Couldn't wait three days. To taste you," Samuel responded. The raw desire in his voice sent a shockwave through me and my cock dribbled, creating a wet spot on the front of my pajamas.

He took a step forward, kicking the door shut behind him with his foot. He started to move on but seemed to think better of it and turned to lock the door, then he carried me down the hallway and into my bedroom, kicking off his shoes.

We hadn't done much in the way of sex since the night in my car other than a few heavy make-out sessions and some hand jobs. I understood, with him just coming to terms with the fact that he was bisexual, that I needed to be patient and give him time to get used to being with a man. I didn't mind giving him that time because he was worth waiting for, but dear Lord, if he didn't at least touch me in the next few minutes, I was going to explode.

Samuel set me down on the bed and I whined in frustration as he pulled away from me. He didn't go far though and I swallowed hard as he reached for his belt, flicking it open and pulling it free of the loops around his waist. I reached for the lamp beside my bed and nearly knocked it over in my rush to turn it on. We'd never been completely naked together and I had to see this.

His bright blue eyes had darkened, and his pupils were blown as he locked eyes with me. The muscles in his arms bulged as he reached over his head and pulled his shirt off. My eyes moved over his chest, greedily eating up the sleek muscles and the smattering of dark fur on his chest. The same dark hair started again just below his navel and traveled down, narrowing into a thin line that taunted me as it disappeared beneath the waistband of his jeans.

I looked up at him, my eyes pleading for more, then I sighed happily as he complied. With a flick of his wrist, his jeans came undone and I saw the tip of his cock peeking out at me over the waistband of his briefs. The thick, mushroomed head was a dark red and he must have approved of me staring at it because a single bead of precum bubbled up from the slit.

I licked my lips eagerly and slid my hand under the elastic of my pajamas, wrapping my hand around my aching cock and giving it a few quick jerks beneath the flimsy material. Samuel did that growly thing that never failed to make me stupid and he quickly dropped his jeans and briefs to the floor and kicked them aside.

I watched as he bent down to pull off his socks and then he was standing in front of me in all his deliciously naked glory. Samuel's skin was tanned, his muscles sleek and well-defined. Free of the restraints of his clothing, his cock jutted out from his body; long and thick. My mouth watered with the need to lick him, suck him, worship his cock, and I had to press the heel of my hand against my own to keep myself from coming too soon.

I reached for the hem of my shirt and quickly slipped it off, letting it drop from my fingers over the side of the bed. Samuel moved to the foot of the mattress and I let out a surprised laugh as he grabbed the legs of my pants and tore them off my body, tossing them over his shoulder, not caring where they landed. My laughter died though as he placed one knee on the bed and slowly began to crawl up and over my body until he was hovering right above me.

He looked into my eyes and then slid his gaze down between our bodies as his hips lowered and our bare cocks rubbed against each other for the first time. We both gasped at the perfect sensation. His eyes darted to mine and they were full of awe and wonder and I felt myself falling even further. He'd had to deny this part of himself for so long and I felt humbled that he trusted me enough to share such an important moment with him.

His strong arms held him up as he looked back down to where we were joined and began to thrust a little faster, the slick of our juices easing his movements. I let him take the lead, doing whatever felt good to him, which in turn felt incredible to me. After a while though I needed more, so I reached between us and grabbed both our cocks in my hand and began stroking them together. When I looked up at him, Samuel's eyes rolled back in his head and his jaw dropped open. Seeing him so completely blissed out urged me on, and I squeezed my hand tighter as my palm moved over our shafts in long, languid strokes.

"Stop!" Samuel cried out after a few minutes, closing one hand over mine to halt my movements. I looked up at him, confused. "If you keep doing that, I'm going to come."

"That's kind of the goal, sweetie," I joked, still not sure why he'd stopped me.

Carefully, he lowered his body onto mine and I shivered as I was suddenly blanketed by his warmth and the smooth texture of his skin. His scent was all around me, a mixture of wood, spice, and arousal and my nostrils flared as I breathed him deep inside my lungs.

"I know, but I was serious before," he told me.

"Umm, you're going to have to remind me of which part because my brain is a bit confuzzled right now." Samuel chuckled, which did amazing things to certain parts of us that were still aligned. I moaned, and he dipped his head and sealed his mouth over mine, biting my bottom lip gently and tugging on it.

"Not. Helping," I panted. He pulled his head back and looked into my eyes. His were clouded with lust but I could also see something else there, like curiosity and longing.

"I was serious when I said I couldn't go three more days without tasting you," he said quietly. My eyes widened, wondering if he meant what I thought he meant, but the answer was made clear with his next words.

"I have no idea what I'm doing, and I may be really terrible at it, but I want to try. I want to know every intimate part of you and I want to bring you the same pleasure that you've brought me." I had to glance down to be sure my body hadn't actually burst into flames and then I stared back at him through heavy lids.

"You won't be terrible at it and you can do whatever you want to me," I whispered.

I held my breath as he began kissing a sensual path down my body. It was clear that he planned on taking his time as he stopped to lave each of my nipples and biting down just enough that I was riding the edge between pleasure and pain. He continued on his path, circling his tongue around my navel and dipping it inside for a taste. Then he lowered even further, settling himself between my spread thighs.

He stopped, spreading my legs even further apart and I lifted my head, so I could see him. He was wearing that same look of awe that he'd had earlier, only this time he was staring at all the most intimate parts of me. I'd been on hundreds of runways with every eye trained on me. My entire career was dependent on people wanting to look at and admire me. But nothing had ever mattered more than having Samuel's focused attention.

His groan let me know that he liked what he saw. Before I knew what was happening, he lowered his head and with the flat of his tongue, licked a wet path up the crease of my thigh. I cried out and my hips jutted off the bed. He laid an arm across my hips, locking me into place as he did the same thing to the other side.

Being held down and completely at this man's mercy as his lips and tongue brought me unthinkable pleasure was fucking with my head and driving me insane. My head tossed back and forth on the pillow and I began to plead for more.

I didn't have to beg for long though before he swiped his tongue over the head of my dick, lapping up my juices with a hungry moan then proceeded to take me into his warm, wet mouth. It was as if all of the desire and questions and fantasies he'd had since he'd first discovered boys were being channeled into that one moment. His movements were a bit frantic, but also enthusiastic, as he tasted and explored, nibbled and sucked until I *thought I would lose my mind.*

My fingers grabbed hold of his hair and my toes curled tightly as I felt my orgasm closing in. I shouted out a warning in case he wanted to pull off, but he refused to stop, doubling his efforts and swallowing my release. The strength of my orgasm stole my breath and it was several minutes before I began to drift back down to earth.

When I was finally able to open my eyes, I gazed down at him. He was staring back at me with a grin and he looked so proud of himself that I couldn't help but laugh. I pulled him up and kissed him hard, savoring the taste of my release on his tongue.

"Now, it's my turn," I said, waggling my brows at him.

"Umm. I already came." He must've read the shock on my face because his face went red and he rushed to explain. "I couldn't help it. I've been dreaming about that for a really long time."

"And how was it?" I asked.

"Even better than I imagined. I have a feeling I'm going to want to do that a lot," he admitted with a grin.

"Far be it from me to deny you anything," I teased.

We took a shower together, changed the sheets then climbed back into bed. I snuggled into his side and his arms wrapped around me as we kissed lazily. I laid my head on his shoulder and gazed up at his profile in the moonlight. He turned his head and looked down at me, a slight crease forming on his forehead. I reached up and ran my finger over it.

"What are you thinking about?"

He hesitated, which made me even more curious. "I was just thinking about the night we met."

"Mmm. That was a very good night. So hot," I murmured, remembering the way we'd watched each other through the window. "What about it specifically though?"

"Well, it's about what you were doing that night. Specifically...the part where you were bottoming," he said.

"You know what bottoming is?"

"Hey, I've done my research," he answered defensively.

"I'm impressed. Now, what about me bottoming had you thinking so hard?"

"I was just wondering...you know...do you always do that?" he asked, sounding adorably embarrassed.

"Not always. I'm actually vers."

"Vers?"

"Versatile. Or a switch as some people call it. Basically, I like it either way. It just depends on my mood and my partner," I explained.

He was quiet for several minutes as he thought things over. "Okay. I think I might want to try both."

My mouth went dry at the thought of being inside Samuel. I guess a small part of me assumed that since he'd only ever been with women he'd want to continue to top. Would there ever come a day when this man didn't surprise me? I hoped not.

"I think that can be arranged. You just let me know when you're ready." I stretched my neck up to kiss him. "Now, I want to hear more about this research you've been doing."

With the noisy plane engine and Korey's deep snores off in the distance, I drifted to sleep and dreamt of my favorite place in the world; Samuel's arms.

FIFTEEN

Samuel

I groaned in frustration, locking my fingers together behind my head to keep from flinging my laptop across the room. I'd spent the last hour trying to do something that should've only taken fifteen minutes. Unfortunately, the Wi-Fi connection in my condo was sketchy at best and my patience had worn thin.

It didn't help that it had been three days since I'd seen Oliver. I knew that his traveling was all part of the job. He had to go to wherever the fashion shows were being held, but that didn't make it any easier to be apart from him. The truth was, I missed him. I missed his laugh and his snarky sense of humor. Most of all, I missed the quiet times we spent together, when we shut the rest of the world out and it was as if we were the only two people in existence. I checked my watch for the hundredth time that evening. Just a few more hours and he'd be home.

Deciding to try and get a little more work done, I attempted to log on one more time. I cheered as I managed to get on successfully, but as soon as I started to type, the connection was lost once again. The sound of someone knocking was the only thing that saved me from following through on my plans to destroy my computer.

Shooting my laptop an angry glare, I pushed away from the table and stood to answer the door.

All of my frustration evaporated the minute I opened the door and found Oliver standing on the other side. Dressed in black slacks and a bright purple silk shirt, with eyeshadow to match and just a hint of pink on his glossy lips, he was literally the most exquisite thing I'd seen since the last time I laid eyes on him.

His eyes lit up and he threw his head back with a surprised laugh as I grabbed him around the waist and pulled him inside, slamming the door and closing us off from the rest of the world. I slid my hands on either side of his face and bent my head for a kiss, backing him up until he was pressed against the door.

Like a starving man, I feasted on his plump lips, eliciting a groan from him that shot straight to my cock. I had only a second to wonder if I was being too rough when his arms wound around my neck and he pulled me even closer, like he never wanted to let me go.

"Surprise," he whispered moments later as we leaned our foreheads together, trying to catch our breath.

I chuckled. "You're early. I didn't think you were supposed to get back for several more hours."

"Complaining?" He tilted his head back and arched a perfectly sculpted eyebrow at me.

"Not at all," I assured him. "I was just going to pick you up at the airport. I even got flowers for the occasion." I smiled as I watched him melt.

"Oh my God! You are the sweetest man ever!" I leaned in for another kiss, but he pulled back with a frown. "Wait! I still want my flowers," he informed me.

I laughed. "Come on, they're in here." We held hands as we walked into the kitchen and only after I'd handed him the bouquet of long-stemmed pink roses was I rewarded with another kiss.

"So, how was your trip?" I asked, leaning my hips against the counter as he checked the cabinets for a glass tall enough to use as a vase.

"The show was incredible and…" He gasped suddenly. I stood up straight and took a step in his direction. I was worried he'd hurt himself on an errant thorn, but he turned to me, wearing a huge smile and laying a hand on his chest. "I got to see her. No, not just see her, I got to *meet* her!" he exclaimed.

I didn't even have to ask which *her* he was referring to. Kate Middleton was all he'd been able to talk about since he'd heard she might attend the show. He began arranging the flowers into the glass as he continued his story.

I tried to listen as he started telling me every detail from what she was wearing, to what was said when they met, but I had trouble paying attention to anything other than how perfect that moment was. Just moments before, I'd been frustrated and miserable and feeling completely out of sorts with him gone and the next, he was standing there in my kitchen filling up the space with his effervescent personality and the light that seemed to shine from within him. I wasn't sure how I'd made it through the first thirty-seven years of my life without him. My world had changed the minute I met Oliver Hughes and I didn't want it to ever go back to what it was before.

"And her shoes were encrusted with thousands of tiny diamonds, can you believe…"

"I love you," I said breathlessly.

Oliver's head whipped around and the flowers he'd been holding dropped to the floor. "What did you say?" he whispered.

I stared straight into his eyes as I answered in a clearer voice that time. "I said, I love you."

His throat bobbed as he swallowed, and his eyes filled with tears and I felt sure that I'd ruined everything. But then he raced forward and threw himself into my arms. I caught him, falling back into the counter and held him as he wrapped his legs around my waist. His hands came up to cradle my face.

"I love you too, Samuel. I love you more than I ever thought I could love someone." My heart felt like it was going to burst out of my chest as he began peppering my face with kisses. I chased his mouth and finally captured his lips with my own.

I carried him into the bedroom and set his feet down on the floor. We took our time removing each other's clothes, kissing each new area of skin as it was revealed to us. As soon as I was naked, I dropped to my knees and I stared up at him as I worked the button through the hole in his pants. His head was tilted downward, and my heart threatened to burst as I saw all of the love and adoration I felt for him reflected back at me. Running his fingers along my jaw, he cupped my chin and lifted it as he bent down to give me a tender kiss.

My fingers curled over the waistband of his pants and began sliding them slowly down his lean legs. He braced a hand on my shoulder as he pulled one leg free then the other, slipping off his heels along the way. I leaned back so I could admire the view, blinking to clear my vision as it grew hazy with lust. Kiss-swollen lips, creamy supple skin, long smooth legs, and the sexiest lacy, purple thong I'd ever seen in my life.

"Holy fuck," I breathed. Oliver was everything; sweet and sassy, saint and sinner all mixed into one unbelievably erotic package.

I felt almost frantic in my need for him and my hands began to shake. I wanted to slam my mouth onto his and drink from his lips. I wanted to run my hands over all that silky skin and feel him responding to my touch. I wanted to strip him down and swallow him whole, driving him out of his mind until I owned each and every one of his whimpers. But it had taken me years to get here, and as much as I wanted all those things, I wanted to take my time more. I wanted to slowly worship every single delectable inch of him.

I leaned forward and ran my nose up the crease of his thigh, breathing in his clean, musky, perfectly unique scent. I heard his breath catch above me and then his hands landed on either side of my head. I nuzzled my cheek back and forth over his lace-covered cock, the stubble along my jaw making a scratchy sound against the fabric.

His legs started to shake, so I told him to sit down then I pressed the palm of my hand to his flat belly until he was lying back on the mattress. Lifting his leg, I gently kissed the arch of his foot and licked over one perfectly manicured toe. Oliver squirmed on the bed, but he didn't try and stop me, so I did the same to the other foot before licking a wet path up his leg. I stopped long enough to show special attention to the delicate skin at the back of his knee, kissing over it and nibbling it with my teeth. Out of the corner of my eye, I saw Oliver's hand slip beneath his panties.

"Uh-uh. That's all mine," I scolded.

"Then you better touch it soon because I'm about to fucking lose my mind," he ground out through clenched teeth.

He didn't have to tell me twice. Kneeling between his legs, I grabbed hold of the flimsy panties and slipped them over his hips and down his legs, tossing them onto the floor in one deft move. He breathed a sigh of relief as I wrapped my hand around his cock and he lifted himself up on his elbows to watch me.

I licked over the wet head, tasting his salty, sweet flavor on my tongue and I reached my hand down around my own cock, giving it a few firm strokes. I opened my mouth wider and began sliding my lips down his long shaft, alternately sucking him off and swirling my tongue around him. His hands landed on my head again, holding me in place as his hips arched off the bed, making his cock slide further down my throat. My head bobbed up and down for several minutes, my wrist twisting along the base of his cock as I coaxed more of his delicious juices from his slit.

He let out a frustrated whimper when I stopped a few minutes later and climbed up and over his body. His eyes were unfocused, and his pupils blown wide with lust and damn if it didn't make me proud that I'd been the one to put that look on his face.

"Why'd you stop?" he whispered, rubbing his thumb over my bottom lip.

"Because I want more tonight," I said softly.

Oliver licked his lips. "We can do as much as you're comfortable with."

I gave him a gentle peck on his lips. "That's the thing. I want it all."

"You want to fuck me?" he asked, a small smile beginning to grow.

My lips brushed over his as I shook my head. "No. I want you to fuck me. I want to feel you moving inside me, baby." I could tell I'd surprised him by the look on his face, but this wasn't a spur-of-the-moment idea for me.

"While you were gone, I did some more research, so I'd know a little more about what to expect. Earlier, I made sure I was prepared. I even spent a little time stretching myself." My face felt hot as I admitted that last part.

Oliver bit his lip. "Oh, fuck, that's hot! Did you get any supplies? I mean, condoms and lube?" I nodded with a smirk. "Well, damn. Aren't you just full of surprises." He grinned.

I jumped off of him and walked around the bed, opening the side table drawer and pulling out the supplies I'd purchased that morning. He slid off the bed and walked over to me, taking the bottle of lube and inspecting the label.

"This is a good brand," he said, sounding impressed.

"Told you I did my research," I said rather smugly.

Oliver laughed. "Okay, smart guy. On the bed." I crawled to the middle of the bed and lay down on my back. "It might be easier on your hands and knees your first time," he suggested, but I shook my head.

"No. I have to see you. I want to be able to look into your eyes," I told him. Oliver's eyes softened, brimming with love for me.

He climbed onto the bed and hovered over me. He smiled at me softly and then kissed me. And oh, God, how he kissed me! It was like a switch had suddenly flipped and he went from being soft, playful Oliver to Take Charge Oliver. My head was spinning, and I was out of breath by the time we ended the kiss.

"I'm going to make you feel so good, honey," he promised. I was still too weak to respond, so I just nodded my head.

I could hear his throaty chuckle as he shifted down the bed. Moments later, my cock was surrounded by a perfect, wet, blinding heat and I let out a guttural moan. Oliver knew just what to do to drive me wild. He licked over the head of my cock and then pursed his lips, blowing cool air over my wet flesh then he swallowed me to the back of his throat, hollowing his cheeks to add suction on the way back up.

"Oliver!" I cried. I wasn't even sure what I was asking for. All I knew was that I didn't want him to hold anything back. I wanted him to do every single thing to me.

As if he heard my thoughts, he lowered his head and licked my sac. His tongue was merciless as he laved my balls, sucking one and then the other into his hot mouth. I gasped as he moved even further down and holding me open with his hands, licked a warm, wet path right over my hole. I'd read about rimming in my research and even seen it done in the little bit of porn I'd watched, but none of that had prepared me for how incredible it would actually feel.

My fingers gripped the sheets, twisting and pulling at them as my brain tried to make sense of the myriad of new sensations. Just as I thought I had a handle on them, Oliver switched things up again by pressing a wet finger to my opening. I tensed at first, but the gentle touch of his hand on my stomach had a calming effect. I breathed in and forced myself to relax.

He pushed his finger in, slowly working me open as his tongue went back to licking around my rim. "I need more," I pleaded a few moments later, reaching a hand down to pull on my cock. Oliver obliged, carefully sliding in another finger and I sighed because it felt even better than before.

"Please, baby, I need to feel you now," I begged.

Oliver climbed to his knees between my legs and reached for the foil packet, tearing it open with his teeth. He watched the hand that was stroking my cock through hooded eyes as he pinched the tip of the condom and slid it down his cock. He grabbed the bottle of lube next. Hearing the click of the cap being opened sent a shiver down my spine and my skin pebbled in anticipation. He made quick work of slicking his cock then rubbed a liberal amount over my pucker.

I hadn't even realized I was holding my breath as he lined the head of his cock up with my hole, but Oliver missed nothing. Placing one hand on the mattress beside my head, he leaned down and looked right into my eyes.

"Are you sure?"

"About this, about you. Yes, I'm sure about all of it," I whispered.

His lips landed on mine and our tongues mated with each other as he slowly pressed inside. The pain was immense, stealing my breath and making my eyes screw tightly shut. I laid a hand on his chest, letting him know that I needed a minute. Oliver leaned his forehead on mine and whispered words of encouragement, and soon, I could feel the tight ring of muscle give way.

His movements were slow and steady, sliding in, inch by blessed inch until he was fully seated inside me. His breathing was labored and sweat dotted the skin above his brow from the strain of holding himself back, but still, he waited patiently until I nodded my head. As the pain gave way, turning into something infinitely more amazing, I began to revel in the feeling of fullness. Knowing that it was Oliver, specifically, who was making love to me made it even better.

The feel of his cock sliding into me and the taste of his tongue on mine soon had my orgasm approaching. I wanted to slow it down, hold off, so I could enjoy this moment for as long as possible, but Oliver was just too skilled and the delicious sensations he was awakening in me were just too much. My grip tightened on my cock and I began jerking off in time with his sure thrusts. I stared up into his eyes and the intensity I saw there made my mouth go dry.

Whether he sensed my orgasm was drawing near or he was about to lose control too, I wasn't sure, but Oliver raised up onto his knees and with a strength I didn't know he possessed, grabbed hold of the back of my thighs and lifted my ass off the bed. The change in angle, had him plunging deeper than before, and suddenly, he hit something inside me that made me feel like I'd touched a live wire.

Fireworks exploded behind my closed lids and I heard myself scream as I came harder than I ever had. Cum sprayed everywhere, hitting my chin and landing on the pillow beside me. In the distance, I heard Oliver shout my name, but it seemed almost dreamlike as I continued to ride the waves of euphoria.

As my head finally began to clear of its fog, I realized Oliver had already pulled out and was lying on top of me. I wrapped my arms around him, kissing the top of his head. My fingers traced lazy figure eights over his back and he made a contented sound in the back of his throat. I couldn't believe how lucky I was to not only get to fall in love with this man, but to have that love returned to me.

After a few minutes, he lifted his head, folding his arms under his chin, and gave me a lazy, sated smile. "You okay?"

"Better than okay." I grinned back.

"You're not too sore?" he asked, his brow scrunching with concern.

I shook my head. "You took perfect care of me, just like I knew you would."

"I love you, Samuel," he whispered.

"I feel like I've been waiting my whole life for you," I answered back.

We shared a long, languid kiss, then Oliver glanced down

between our bodies. "We're a bit of a mess. Care to join me in the shower?"

"Love to." We climbed out of bed and I grimaced at the stretched feeling in my ass. Oliver noticed the look on my face and laughed.

"Don't worry. It'll go back to normal." I felt sure I was imagining the smugness in his tone.

"Well, I figured one thing out for sure," I told him as we stepped into the bathroom. I reached in and started the shower while he disposed of the condom.

"What's that?"

"I'm definitely a switch."

"Is that right?" Oliver said, pressing himself up against my back and wrapping his arms around my waist. "Maybe we should try it both ways, just to be sure."

"It's the responsible thing to do," I teased as I pulled him into the shower behind me. "I definitely want to try bottoming again too though. Only I want something a little different next time," I informed him seriously.

"Oh, yeah? And what's that?"

"Wear your heels."

"Fuuuuck."

SIXTEEN

Oliver

"**M**orning, baby," Samuel said as he walked into my office carrying two steaming mugs.

We'd spent every night together since I'd come back from London and I had to admit, seeing a sleep-rumpled Samuel first thing in the morning was quickly becoming more addictive than the coffee he held in his hands. With no shirt on and his sleep pants riding low on his hips, I wanted to trace that thin line of hair that disappeared right under the waistband with my tongue. That morning, however, I was too distracted to enjoy the view.

I held a shaky finger up to him as I finished listening to the person on the other end of the phone. Samuel's forehead wrinkled, a look of concern crossing his features as he noticed my distress. He set the mugs down on the desk and quickly walked behind me, bending down and kissing the top of my head as he wrapped his arms around my chest. I placed one hand on his strong forearm and squeezed. The feel of having him near was the only thing holding me together at that point.

"Are you absolutely sure?" I asked weakly. I listened to the man's reply. "Okay. Thank you very much for your time." I ended the call and threw my phone down on my desk. Leaning forward, I buried my face in my hands, my fingers digging into my scalp. I felt like I'd been sucker punched.

"What's wrong, baby? You're scaring me." Samuel swung my chair around and knelt in front of me, pulling my hands away from my face so he could see me. His hands cupped my jaw as his blue eyes raked over me.

"Oh, God, Samuel, I trus...tru...trusted..." My eyes swam with tears that had started to spill over and I knew I probably wasn't making any sense, but I just couldn't manage to spit the poisonous truth out. Throwing my arms around him, I buried my face in his neck and cried, big wracking sobs that felt like they were being torn straight from the depths of my soul. I'd never felt so violated, betrayed or so utterly stupid in my entire life.

Samuel wrapped me up in his arms and hugged me tightly, letting me unburden myself on him. When I was all cried out, I leaned back, swiping the tears that had gathered on my lashes. He handed me a tissue and I blew my nose. His eyes were full of love and compassion and not for the first time, I thanked God for bringing him into my life.

"Talk to me, baby."

I drew in a ragged breath and started from the beginning, telling him about my credit card being declined at the coffee shop, Korey's moodiness and his increasing push for me to work harder, longer days. Samuel listened to all of it without interrupting. If I hadn't already memorized every single inch of him, I might have missed the subtle tightening around his mouth or the hard edge his eyes had begun to take.

"Korey's seemed so stressed lately, so I figured I'd look into it instead of adding even more to his plate. But when I called the card company, they said I was over my limit. I told him that was impossible because I have a really high limit and I rarely use that card. He read off some of the higher-priced purchases done recently and

I just knew. I called the other card companies and found out they were all over or near their limit as well." My eyes welled up with fresh tears and Samuel squeezed my hands as they rested in my lap.

"That was the bank manager I was talking to when you came in. He let me know that my account is empty. That was my life savings, Samuel. That money was there so I could buy a home one day and to use for my retirement, but it's all gone. It's all gone and I'm to my eyeballs in debt because Korey's been stealing from me." Tears ran freely down my cheeks. I could feel the anger rolling off of him in waves, but his touch remained gentle as he brushed them away with his thumbs.

"Why would he do this, Samuel? I thought he cared about me. I thought he was my friend." I looked at him imploringly, hoping he would be able to make sense of this mess; wanting him to find some other explanation for how this could've happened that didn't end in Korey betraying me. But the look on his face told me he couldn't do that, and I started to cry again.

"I'm so stupid," I mumbled.

"Hey, don't say that!" Samuel scolded.

"It's true!" I insisted, brushing my tears away angrily and standing up so I could pace. "If I hadn't let him put his name on those accounts, he never would've been able to get to that money. I was stupid and naïve and now, there's nothing I can do about it because technically he didn't steal anything. As far as the bank and credit card companies are concerned, those were shared accounts and the money belonged to Korey as much as it did to me."

"Listen to me," Samuel said, catching hold of my arm and turning me to face him. "Your only mistake was in trusting the wrong person. You aren't responsible for Korey's actions, only he is. He took you under his wing and made you believe that he had your best interests at heart. And he followed through on his promise to get your career up and running, so you had no reason to doubt his sincerity. The fact that he took advantage of that trust is on him and he'll pay for it."

I arched a brow at him. "I don't usually like to wield this around, but the situation sort of calls for it this time. My agency was featured in Forbes magazine last year as one of the leading privately owned advertising agencies in the country. I hold a certain amount of clout and I have a lot of connections in the fashion industry. All I have to do is make a few phone calls and Korey Duncan will be a pariah, a laughing stock. No one will want to work with him ever again."

I shivered at his growly, possessive tone and I idly thought that I wouldn't mind seeing that dominant attitude in the bedroom occasionally. Samuel was full of surprises, but one thing that didn't surprise me was how protective he was of those he loved. It just so happened that the list of people he loved now included me. My heart filled with love and gratitude for this man. I'd grown stronger over the last few years. I knew that I could've handled this situation on my own if needed, but with Samuel by my side, I didn't have to.

I slid my arms around his waist and rested my head on his shoulder. His arms circled around me and he kissed the side of my face. I was angry and hurt by what Korey did, but I wouldn't allow him to destroy me. Sure, it would suck having to dig myself out of the financial hole Korey had created, but thankfully, I had a lot of money tucked away in other private accounts that would get me through while I worked to rebuild. A few extra modeling shoots each month, and I'd eventually have those cards paid off.

"I know this has been quite a shock to you, but we shouldn't wait too long to confront him," he said carefully, probably afraid of sending me falling into another fit of tears. I was done crying, for the moment at least. I had business to take care of. I could fall apart later.

Picking up my phone, I fired off a quick text then turned to Samuel. "We need to get dressed. Korey will be here in an hour. I figured we shouldn't meet somewhere public. If things go the way I expect them to go…well, let's just say, the tabloids aren't the kind of magazines I want to be on the cover of. Plus, it won't hurt that we'll have the home court advantage."

"Have I ever told you how brilliant you are?" He gave me a proud grin.

Exactly an hour later, a knock on the door sent my heart into my throat. Regardless of how pissed I was, I was still nervous about how this was all going to go down. I laid a hand on the doorknob then glanced over my shoulder. Samuel stood just a few steps away, looking formidable with his arms crossed and a firm set to his jaw. He sent me a quick wink which settled something inside me and I twisted the handle, confident that no matter what happened, he would always have my back.

Korey smiled as I opened the door and held up a white takeout bag. "I brought some of those little pastries you were eyeing at that French restaurant. I figured we could go over the schedule. I know you said you wanted to cut back, but I got you a contract…" His words trailed off as he stepped inside and noticed Samuel standing there. "Sorry. I didn't realize you had a friend over or I would've brought more pastries."

I tilted my head at him, feeling like I was truly seeing him for the first time. Gone were the rose-colored glasses that had only let me see with blind trust, gratitude and maybe even a hint of hero worship. I was wearing clearer lenses now and they were able to reveal all the lies, the manipulation and the greed that surrounded Korey Duncan.

"Have a seat. We need to talk." My tone must've alerted him to the fact that something wasn't right because his eyes narrowed.

"What's this about?" he asked, bristling a bit.

"Oh, I'm pretty sure you know what it's about, but why don't you take a seat and tell us what you did with my money?"

His face was almost comical; eyes bulging as they darted back and forth between me and Samuel, jaw dropping and sweat pebbling up on his forehead. Turning to me, he held his hands up in a placating gesture.

"Oliver, sweetheart…"

"You don't get to call him that!" Samuel's words cut through the air like a whip being cracked; sharp, painful, and leaving a stinging mark on its intended target.

Korey's jaw clenched as he glared at Samuel, but then he turned to me. "Oliver, I'm sure this is all very confusing, but I can explain…"

"That's great, because I'd love for you to explain to me how my entire savings is gone or how I got to be over six hundred thousand dollars in debt. Can you explain to me what you used the money for or why you thought you had the right to touch something that didn't belong to you?" His eyes widened, clearly not expecting me to stand up to him that way.

"Does this have something to do with him?" he sneered, pointing at Samuel. "Is he the one feeding you all these lies?"

"They're not lies, Korey. I already spoke with the bank and the credit card companies and they confirmed everything," I said, surprised at how calm my voice sounded when inside, I was shaking like a damn earthquake.

"Fine. I admit it. I skimmed some money from you." Samuel barked out a humorless laugh and Korey shot him a look, searing with hate. He turned back to me again. "Look, I'll repay what I took. You can take some from each of my checks until it's all back again. Okay?"

Samuel and I both shot him incredulous looks. Did he really think he was going to be able to pay back the money and I'd forget about everything else? Did he really think the money was the only thing that mattered? The answer to that question was swift and painful and my earlier bravado was replaced with overwhelming sadness. I'd thought Korey was my friend, that he cared about me, but I was never anything more than a dollar sign to him.

"You're fired, Korey," I murmured. The look Samuel gave me was full of sad understanding. He knew how painful this was for me.

"What the hell do you mean, I'm fired? You can't fire me. I created you! You were a nobody when I met you and without me, you'll go back to being a nobody," he roared, face mottled with rage.

"Yeah, okay. That's enough out of you." Korey twisted and turned, trying to get Samuel off him as he grabbed him by the arm and hauled him toward the door.

"Get your hands off me!" Korey screamed.

"Out you go!" Samuel said as he opened the door and tossed Korey outside.

"This isn't over!" Korey started to yell, but his words were cut off as Samuel slammed the door in his face, twisting the lock in place.

He turned around with a satisfied grin, but as soon as he saw that I was shaking, he came running over and wrapped me up in his arms. "What can I do, baby? What do you need?"

I felt cold all over and my teeth were starting to chatter. "I just need you. I need you to hold me."

Samuel bent and with one arm behind my back and the other under my legs, lifted me in a cradled position. He carried me down the hallway and laid me on the bed, quickly undressing me until I was just in my underwear. He did the same with his own clothes and then he helped us both under the covers. He curled around me and I could feel the heat from his body seeping through me, all the way to the bone. We lay there quietly, waiting for the shaking to subside.

"What happens now?" I asked wearily.

"We'll find you another agent. One that understands that you're in charge. You set the rules and you choose your own schedule," he said firmly. I smiled softly, liking that idea.

"What do you think will happen to Korey?" Whether or not

our friendship had ever meant anything to him, it had been real to me and it was hard to just switch that off and make myself stop caring about him.

Samuel sighed. "I suppose he'll crawl under a rock for a while, lick his wounds and figure out where to go from there. I know you truly cared about him, so I won't do anything just yet, but if he tries anything funny or I hear that he's slandering your name, I'll go after him and he will not like the outcome."

I pulled his chin down for a kiss. "I love you," I whispered. He might have said he loved me back, but I was already falling asleep.

It was several hours before I woke again. Samuel was sitting beside me in the bed, his back resting against the headboard and his tablet in his hands. I took a moment to admire him. The sheets were pooled around his waist, leaving miles of smooth tanned skin on display, except for the perfect amount of fur that covered his pecs. His jaw was strong, his bottom lip fuller than the top and the silver flecks in his hair still did crazy things to my heart. He was every fantasy I'd ever had brought to life, and the pair of black-rimmed reading glasses he was wearing were just icing on the cake.

"Hey, sweetheart. How are you?" he asked, setting his tablet aside. He scooted down in the bed and I curled into his side, breathing in the smell of his skin.

"My head's pounding and I feel like I've gone a few rounds with a heavyweight champ. Other than that, I'm great," I joked lamely. Samuel gave me a sympathetic smile and began rubbing my head. I groaned as his fingernails scratched over my scalp, easing the sharp pain in my head until it had settled into a dull throb.

"I need to email all the photographers and designers I work with on a regular basis and let them know to contact me directly instead of going through Korey. I'm not looking forward to it. I'm sure they'll have a lot of questions, but I'll feel better once I get that part out of the way," I said with a sigh.

Samuel pressed his lips to mine in a tender kiss. "Why don't you work on that while I make us something to eat and then we can take a long hot bath together."

"Mmmm. That sounds perfect," I murmured against his lips. He kissed me again and then started to pull away, but I grabbed his wrist to stop him. "Thank you. For everything."

A warm smile lifted the corners of his mouth. "You don't have to thank me. I love you and I would do anything for you." He pressed another kiss to my mouth and I melted into the sheets, then he stood and sauntered out of the bedroom.

A half hour later, I was still on the phone. I'd sent an email to the people I worked with most often and right away, a few of them had called to check on me. It was nice to see that so many of them cared and that what had happened wouldn't have a negative impact on our working relationships. If anything, most of them seemed a little relieved that they wouldn't have to deal with Korey anymore, which made me wonder how much had been happening behind the scenes that I wasn't aware of. Of course, I was all too aware of Ben's disdain for the man, a fact that he didn't bother hiding when he'd called a few minutes before.

"I never did like him," he exclaimed vehemently. "The guy's never been anything but a pompous asshole who thought he was better than everyone else."

"Apparently everyone else was able to see his true colors except for me," I said glumly.

"Yeah, well, take it from me, people only let you see the parts of themselves they want you to see."

"I suppose you're right," I said with a sigh.

"But hey, we can have even more fun now, and Korey won't be able to bother you ever again," he said gently.

"Thanks, Ben. I appreciate that and I'm really glad you called."

"Anytime. I'll always be here for you. I can even come over if you want some company."

I started to reply when Samuel peeked his head through the

doorway. "Dinner's ready," he whispered when he saw I was on the phone.

"I've got to go, Ben. Samuel's got dinner ready."

"Oh! I didn't realize you were still seeing him," he said.

"Yeah, he's a great guy. I'm very lucky to have him," I said, smiling at Samuel who was still lingering near the door. He pointed to his chest as if to say, "who me?" and I nodded my head slowly, licking over my bottom lip in the way that drove him wild. His eyes darkened, and he took a step forward. "Uh, I've really gotta go, Ben. I'll talk to you later."

I didn't even wait for his reply before ending the call and tossing my phone on the desk. My last thought before Samuel closed in on me and I lost the ability to think, was that dinner was going to have to wait.

SEVENTEEN

Samuel

"**A**re you sure I look okay?" Oliver asked for what seemed like the twentieth time since we got in the car to head to the restaurant. He pulled the visor down and opened the mirror, so he could inspect his makeup, wiping his fingertip along the edge of his lips.

I reached over and took his hand, bringing it to my mouth for a kiss. "Baby, quit worrying. They're going to love you almost as much as I do," I assured him.

I'd called Brooklyn the week before just to check in and see how she was doing. Our relationship was important to both of us and so we'd each been making an effort to keep up with all the new things going on in our life; her with school and me with my new relationship. While we talked, I'd told her my plan for celebrating Gayle's birthday. I offered to fly Brooklyn in for the evening, so we could take Gayle to dinner at her favorite restaurant then I'd send the two of them off for a luxury spa weekend. Brooklyn had loved the idea and I was excited to get to see her. I was so grateful that our relationship seemed to have weathered the storm it'd been put through.

Gayle and I had discussed it and even though we wanted to introduce our daughter to the new men in our lives and them to her, neither of us wanted to push the issue. We knew Brooklyn was still adjusting to the fact that her parents were no longer married, much less that we were both seeing new people. She needed time. We agreed to let Brooklyn set the pace, trusting that she would let us know when she was ready to take that next step.

So, she'd completely thrown me for a loop when she suggested inviting both Andrew and Oliver to the birthday dinner. It had taken me several seconds before I could speak around the lump in my throat. I'd finally choked out a thank you. "You and Mom are important to me. I figured I should get to know the people that are important to you," she'd said softly. Those words meant more to me than she could ever know. It proved to me that we were really going to be okay, perhaps even better than before.

Oliver, of course, had been stunned by the invitation, but just as touched by my daughter's gesture as I was. He'd spent all week asking me questions, wanting to know everything he possibly could about the two women in my life. But as the time got closer, his nerves had started to get the best of him until he'd turned into the frantic, rapidly speaking, adorable mess beside me.

"But what if they don't? What if they take one look at me and decide I'm not good enough for you? What if they think I'm too young or not sophisticated enough? Oh, God! What if we sit there the whole time and can't think of anything to talk about!" he said, nearing hysteria.

I'd started to laugh but stopped when I saw his face and realized how serious he was. It didn't matter where we went, Oliver could make friends with anyone. He even knew that the lady who worked at the post office was expecting her third grandchild in a month. I'd been with him when she pulled him aside to show him the sonogram pictures. I couldn't imagine a scenario where he wouldn't know what to say.

"Honey, I promise you that everything will be just fine. I've already told them a lot about you and you know all about them. I'm sure you'll find stuff to talk about and if not, I'll be there to help steer the conversation. Besides, you aren't the only one in the hot seat tonight. We're all meeting Andrew for the first time too," I reminded him.

"Oh! That's right. That definitely makes me feel better," he said, exhaling deeply. "Okay, new plan. If things start to go wonky, we throw Andrew under the bus and ask him what his intentions are with your ex-wife," he joked. He squeezed my hand. "I'm sorry. I know I've been acting like a crazy person today. This is just huge, you know? They're important to you, so I really want them to like me."

"I get it. I really do, but all you have to do is be yourself and there's no way they won't fall in love with you. After all, I did." Oliver leaned across the armrest to kiss my cheek and then rested his head on my shoulder with a contented sigh.

One positive thing about him focusing so much attention on meeting Brooklyn and Gayle was that it had helped to keep his mind off of what had happened with Korey. So far, things had been fairly peaceful. We hadn't seen or heard anything from Korey since I'd tossed him out that day, but I had several friends and colleagues keeping their eyes and ears open in case he tried anything. One false move and I would end things for him. I wasn't about to let Oliver be hurt by that man ever again.

I pulled up in front of the restaurant and handed my keys to the valet, then went around to the other side of the car to open the door for my date. As always, he looked stunning, but I had to admit that seeing him in his sleek black suit, black shirt and fuchsia tie with eyeshadow to match, was making me have some very inappropriate thoughts. Inappropriate for having dinner with my ex-wife and teenage daughter anyway. I sighed loudly just thinking how difficult it was going to be to try and get through dinner while keeping my hands to myself.

"What were you just thinking, Mr. Bishop?" he purred, looking up at me with a knowing smirk.

I leaned down and whispered in his ear so no one else would hear. "If you must know, Mr. Hughes, I was just thinking that maybe later, I would peel that suit off of you and we could put that tie to better use."

A soft whimper escaped his glossy pink lips and I responded with a growl. Being with Oliver had awakened desires in me that I hadn't known existed before. It seemed like the more sex we had, the more I wanted. Sometimes, I wondered if I was trying to make up for all those years that I'd missed out on knowing the pleasures of a man's body, but then it also could've been that for the first time, I was madly and passionately in love with someone. Perhaps it was a combination of the two, but either way, I wouldn't have wanted to be with anyone other than Oliver. He was truly perfect for me in every way.

To anyone else walking by, it would've appeared as if he were simply fixing my tie for me. Only I was privy to the subtle tug he gave the material or the way his eyes darkened to a deep russet color. "We better get in and find our table before I drag you into the bathroom of this very respectable establishment and drop to my knees for you." With that, he smoothed his hands down my tie, turned, and walked away. I stood there, trying to remember how to breathe until he called out my name. "You...coming?" I turned to see him holding the door open, a proud smile gracing his lips.

With a low growl, I followed him into the restaurant where I gave my name to the maître d'. Oliver gave me a panicked look when the man informed us that the rest of our party had already arrived. He latched onto my hand and I gave it a reassuring squeeze, keeping hold of him as the maître d' led us to our table.

Brooklyn saw us first and she stood, making her way around the table to greet us. "Hi, Daddy," she said happily as she hugged me. I drew her into my arms and hugged her back.

"Hi, sweetheart. You look gorgeous." She'd always been a pretty girl but being out on her own had changed her into a beautiful young woman, full of confidence and grace.

"Thank you. And you just keep getting more handsome each time I see you."

I turned to Oliver who'd been watching us intently. "Honey, I want you to meet my…Oliver." I wasn't sure how to finish that sentence because we'd never really put a label on what we were to each other, but I decided that *my Oliver* fit just perfectly so I left it at that.

Brooklyn laughed as she turned to Oliver. "Hi, his Oliver. I'm his Brooklyn," she teased and then gave him a gentle hug. I could see his face over her shoulder and he looked startled at first, but then he smiled and hugged her back.

"It's really nice to meet you. Your dad has told me so much about you." My heart gave a flip as I stood there, grinning like a loon. The two people I loved most in the world were finally in one place, meeting for the first time. And it was going well.

When I turned my head, I saw Gayle watching me with a peaceful, happy look on her face and I wondered if she'd been thinking the same thing when she'd introduced our daughter to Andrew. I walked over and gave her a hug, wished her a happy birthday and then turned to the man seated next to her. Andrew was a handsome man with a genuine smile and kind eyes. The way he looked at Gayle when she introduced the two of us, as if the sun rose and set just for her, made me like him immediately.

I finished introducing Oliver to everyone, blushing profusely when Gayle whispered to him, loud enough for me to hear, "Hang on tight to him. He's one of the best." He turned and gave me a quick perusal.

"Yeah, I know he is." The smile on his face was warm and sweet and I returned it with one of my own.

"Okay, you guys. That's enough," Brooklyn scolded, pointing

at all four of us. "You're still my parents. I don't need to see you guys making googly eyes at each other." When she wrinkled her nose we all started laughing.

The rest of dinner went much the same, with good food, wine, and lots of lighthearted banter. Andrew and I discovered that we both shared a passion for basketball, his eyes nearly bugged out of his head when I told him my company had season tickets and that I'd give him a set whenever he wanted to go.

"Careful now, you keep offering stuff like that and he'll start liking you more than he does me," Gayle joked, making us all laugh.

Gayle commented that she loved Oliver's makeup and Brooklyn shyly admitted that she bragged to her friends at school about her dad dating a supermodel. That part took me by surprise. I had no idea that Brooklyn had told any of her friends, but the fact that she had proved to me that she really was okay with everything.

Oliver, of course, was his usual charming self, just as I knew he would be, and soon he had everyone at the table eating out of the palm of his hand. Brooklyn and Gayle gushed over his hair and makeup and hung on his every word as he told them about the time he met Kate Middleton. In fact, they got along so well that before we left, they made him promise they'd all go shopping the next time Brooklyn was back in town.

"You okay? You've been awfully quiet," Oliver said as we drove back to his place.

"Yeah, sorry. I guess I was just lost in thought."

"Care to share?"

I shrugged my shoulders. "I was just thinking about how lucky I am. Not only are Gayle and I still friends, but my relationship with Brooklyn is stronger than it ever was. But the best part is having you in my life. You make me happier than I've ever been, and I'm so in love with you. Seeing the three of you getting along so well tonight just made me realize that I really do have everything I could ever want."

"I can see why you love them so much, they're absolutely wonderful and they couldn't have been any nicer to me. But you're not the only lucky one. Meeting you was the best thing that ever happened to me. You make me feel happier, safer, and more loved than I've ever been." He lifted my hand that was resting in his lap and brought it to his mouth, giving each fingertip a delicate kiss.

We drove for several miles without talking, both of us enjoying the other's company while a romantic song played softly through the speakers. In my head, I was already making plans for getting him home and making slow, sweet love to him. The sound of his phone ringing broke through the quiet, making us both jump. We laughed as he pulled it from his pocket and looked at the screen, but then his forehead scrunched.

"Who is it?" I asked.

"I don't know. It's not a number I recognize," he said as he hit the green button with his thumb. Curious, I listened in to his side of the conversation, broken by pauses as he listened to whoever was on the line. "Hello? Speaking, who is this?" He looked over at me, his face showing concern as he listened. "What's this about? Okay, I'm actually not too far away right now. I can be there in a few minutes. Yeah, see you then."

"What was that about?" I asked as he shoved his phone back in his pocket.

"I have no idea. That was the police, calling from one of the nearby stations. They said they need to speak to me, but when I asked what it was about, they wouldn't say. They just told me to get there as soon as possible." His face had started to go pale. "Do you think it could have something to do with Korey? Do you think he's trying to start trouble of some kind?"

I grabbed his hand and held onto it. "I have no idea, but I can't imagine it would be Korey. You did absolutely nothing wrong and he knows it. Either way, you won't have to deal with it alone."

"Thank you," he said weakly and I ground my teeth together.

I didn't say it out loud because Oliver was already stressed enough, but if it was Korey trying to cause him problems, I was going to kill him.

We pulled into the parking lot of the police station a few minutes later and I held his hand as we walked inside. The man behind the desk glared at us over the top of his reading glasses, seeming particularly put out by having to put his crossword puzzle away to help us.

"Can I help you?" he asked in a bored voice.

"Uh, yes, sir. I received a phone call a few minutes ago from a Detective Rogers. He asked me to come in, so he could speak to me," Oliver explained politely.

"Name?" the man asked in that same droll voice.

"Oliver Hughes."

"Have a seat and wait while I call back…"

"That's okay, Ted, I'm right here," said a deep voice.

A second later, a man came around the corner. He was tall and handsome, but his face looked tired and drawn as he looked up from the open file he was carrying in his hands. He frowned as he looked at Oliver and I stiffened next to him, ready to come to his defense if the guy was going to be an asshole. He seemed to shake off whatever was bothering him though and stepped forward to shake our hands.

"I'm Detective Rogers. Thank you for coming in so quickly."

"This is my boyfriend, Samuel Bishop," Oliver said as the detective and I shook hands.

"Nice to meet you. Why don't we go back to my office, so we can talk privately?"

Oliver shot me a nervous look, so I laid my hand on his lower back as we followed the detective down a narrow hallway. When we reached the last door on the right, the detective opened it and told us to go on in.

"If you'll both excuse me for just a minute, I want to ask one of my colleagues to sit in with us while we talk. Please, have a seat. I'll be right back." He was back out the door before we could say another word.

We exchanged bewildered looks but sat down in the two chairs across from the desk. I stared at a framed photo on the desk of what I assumed was the detective's family. He had a beautiful wife and three younger kids. He looked relaxed and happy in the photo, much different from the tense man we'd just met. *I suppose dealing with the worst of society every day will do that to a person.*

I turned my head quickly when Oliver gasped beside me. His face had lost all color and his eyes were huge as he stared up at the wall to the right of the desk. I followed the direction he was looking, and a cold chill swept down my body as I took in what had spooked him.

I recognized several of the young men from their news stories. They were the victims of the serial killer that had been terrorizing Los Angeles for months, but there were three other faces that I didn't recognize.

"Jesus," I breathed as we looked over the photos the news hadn't shown. The crime scene photos that were much too gruesome for public viewing.

The similarities between the victims and their deaths were chilling to say the least, making it obvious that the killer had a *type.* As the news had reported, all of them were male, young, probably in their early twenties, with blond hair. They all had the same bruising around their necks and some of the close-up images showed the perfect outline of fingers, some even showing stitching marks along the skin which made me wonder if the killer had worn gloves.

"Sorry." We both jumped at the sound of Detective Rogers' voice. He indicated to the wall of photos. "I didn't mean to leave you here with those, that was thoughtless. This is my partner, Detective Billings," he said, gesturing over his shoulder to a shorter, middle-aged man. Detective Billings ignored me all together, but he took one glance at Oliver and then exchanged a wild-eyed look with his partner.

"What's going on? Why did you need to speak to Oliver?" I asked, addressing Detective Rogers as he sat down at his desk. Detective Billings closed the door, then rested his back against it with his arms crossed.

"I'm getting to that and I appreciate your patience so far. I just need to ask you a few questions before I get to why you're here." I watched Detective Rogers as he laid the closed file he'd been carrying on his desk.

"Okay," Oliver murmured.

"Wait, should he have a lawyer present if you're going to question him?" I asked, already pulling my phone out of my pocket.

"No, that won't be necessary. We don't suspect him of any wrongdoing," he assured me. "Oliver, I understand you're a professional model, is that correct?"

"Yes," he answered, clearly confused about where the conversation was heading. He wasn't the only one.

"And can you tell me your relationship to a Mr. Korey Duncan?" Oliver and I both stiffened, drawing the attention of the detective whose eyes darted back and forth between us.

"Korey was my agent."

"Was?" Detective Rogers asked, missing nothing.

Oliver nodded. "I fired him recently when I found out he'd been stealing money from me."

The detective's eyebrows scrunched. "Did you report the crime?"

"No. His name was on the accounts, so technically, he didn't break the law. But it was my money and he broke my trust. I couldn't continue to work with him after that," Oliver explained. I laid my hand on his back, responding to the still fresh pain in his voice.

"When did you fire him?"

"It was a little over a week ago," Oliver responded miserably. I could see him shutting down the longer the questioning continued, and it was starting to piss me off.

"And have you tried to see or get in touch with him since?"

"No, neither of us have, and frankly, we don't want to. Now, will you please tell us what's going on? Is Korey trying to start problems for Oliver?" I cut in.

Detective Rogers shared another mysterious look with his partner and then turned his attention back on us. "No, Korey Duncan's not trying to start anything. He's dead."

EIGHTEEN

Samuel

D etective Rogers got the trash can over the desk and in front of Oliver just in time. I could feel the muscles in his back clenching under the palm of my hand as he heaved violently, expelling everything he'd eaten that day. I hadn't noticed Detective Billings leaving the room until he appeared back through the door- way carrying a cup of water and a wad of fresh paper towels.

I mumbled a quick thank you and laid a wet paper towel on the back of Oliver's neck. As his heaving turned into quiet sobs, I used the other paper towels to wipe his face while whispering soothing words. I'd been so focused on taking care of him, I hadn't noticed how badly my own hands were shaking until I went to hand him the water. He swished a little around in his mouth and then spit into the trash can. When I was sure he wasn't going to be sick anymore, I handed the trash can off to Detective Billings who took it out of the room. Then I wrapped an arm around Oliver and he cuddled into me, burying his face in my shoulder.

"Come on, baby. Let me take you home," I murmured.

"I can't let you do that."

"Look, he just found out that someone he thought was his

friend until very recently has died and he's very upset. Let me take him home and I'll bring him back in the morning to answer any questions you have," I hissed.

"I understand, but I can't let you leave just yet," Detective Rogers stated calmly.

"Why the hell not? You said yourself you don't suspect him of any wrongdoing. That means he's free to leave," I argued.

"Yes, he's free to leave, but I need you to hear me out first. There's a lot more going on here that you don't know. Hell, we didn't even know until you showed up here." I glared at the man sitting across from me.

"It's okay. Let's hear what they have to say," Oliver whispered.

I put a finger under his chin and lifted his face, so I could see him. His eyes were red-rimmed, his cheeks streaked with salt and every so often a gentle hiccup would escape from his lips. He looked so sad and vulnerable and all I wanted to do was take him home and hold him close.

"Baby, you don't have to do this right now. We can come back first thing in the morning."

"It won't hurt any less then. I'd rather just get this over with, so we can go home and stay there," Oliver told me, his eyes etched with pain. I kissed his forehead and then nodded.

"What do you need from us, Detective?" he asked.

Detective Rogers opened the file in front of him and then looked back at us. "Have either of you been following the serial killer case in the news?"

Oliver nodded. "A little."

"Some," I answered.

"Well, Detective Billings and I are the lead investigators assigned to the case. There are several things that you may not know, some things we've kept out of the public eye on purpose. There are a couple of victims who haven't yet been identified, therefore, their families have not been notified. We also don't like to show our hand too much when dealing with a very intelligent and very violent sociopath. The more information is leaked out, the more we give away any good leads we may have and the harder it'll be to catch this guy. The things I'm going to tell you two need to stay in this room, understood?" Oliver and I shared a confused look but nodded our heads in agreement.

"Good. Now, as you can tell from the photos on the wall, there are three more victims than what's been reported by the news. Those three were found recently, but from the level of decomposition, we've determined the oldest to have been killed as far back as two years ago. Considering that this has been going on awhile and three of the murders just took place over the last several months, we have reason to believe that either there are a lot more victims that haven't been found yet or things are escalating with this psycho. Maybe even both. Each one of them are Caucasian, male, blond, and between the ages of nineteen and twenty-six. They were each killed in the exact same way too. Strangulation."

"I'm sorry, Detective. This is all horrific and extremely sad, but what does this have to do with Korey's death or us for that matter?" Oliver interjected.

"Because your friend was murdered in the same fashion," Detective Billings answered.

Oliver gasped. "Korey was strangled?"

"Yes," Detective Rogers confirmed. "Normally, we wouldn't have put his case together with the serial murders since he doesn't fit the physical description of the other victims, but as you can imagine, we're looking even more closely into every homicide right now. Especially those involving strangulation. Korey's body was discovered this afternoon inside a dumpster. His wallet was still in his back pocket. That's how we were able to identify him. The business cards inside the wallet named him as your agent which is why we called you. We honestly just brought you in here tonight to see if you could shed any light as to who might want him dead or why.

But then we got a look at you and we believe we might have found our first real solid lead."

"What do you mean?" Oliver asked. The feeling of dread that I'd been experiencing since Oliver first got the phone call now settled in my stomach like a giant rock.

Detective Billings moved forward and sat on the edge of his partner's desk. His voice was gentle when he spoke to Oliver. "All of the victims match your physical description and now your former agent shows up dead, murdered in the exact same way, not long after you discovered that he betrayed you and severed all ties with him. It's way too much to be a coincidence. We believe you're the link. The thing that this serial killer is after." Blood rushed through my ears at the detective's last words and my head began to spin. This couldn't be happening. Oliver, my sweet Oliver, couldn't be the target of a serial killer.

"Oliver, is there anyone you can think of that's been acting oddly around you? Anyone hanging around you more? Showing up in strange places or getting a little too friendly, lately?" Detective Rogers asked.

Oliver's face scrunched as he gave the questions consideration. "I can't think of anyone. I work with a lot of different people each week, but most of them are ones that I've worked with for years and have good relationships with. They're all respectful and professional."

"What about around your home?"

He shook his head. "I live in an apartment building and don't even know a lot of my neighbors. Oh! There is this one guy who's always staring at me when I come home. He's pretty creepy." The detectives each perked up at the information, but then deflated with Oliver's next words. "But he's in his eighties or something and has to use a cane to get around. And he only has one arm."

"Okay, so probably not him then," Detective Billings said. I noticed the slight twitch of his lips as he struggled not to laugh in what was otherwise a very serious situation.

"What about at any clubs or parties you've been to recently?" Detective Rogers suggested hopefully.

Oliver and I exchanged a look and his eyes softened. "Just this guy, but he loves me too much to ever hurt me." I gave him a warm smile, so happy that when everything else was falling apart around him, he knew that he could still trust me.

"Was there anyone that Korey didn't get along with?"

Oliver snorted. "That would take all night." Detective Billings' eyebrows shot up. "I spoke with the various magazine editors, photographers, and designers that I work with most often to let them know that Korey and I were no longer working together and that they needed to contact me for any jobs they had coming up instead of him. Every single one of them told me how relieved they were to not have to deal with him anymore. Apparently, Korey had a real knack for rubbing people the wrong way. Even my newest photographer, Greg, couldn't stand him, and they only worked together a couple of times."

Detective Rogers reached into his desk drawer and pulled out a pad of paper and a pen and handed them both to Oliver. "Would you mind making a list of those individuals? I don't want to leave any stone unturned."

Oliver took the pen and paper and began writing out the list of names. When he was finished, he handed it back to the detective. He let out a jaw-cracking yawn then and sagged his body against mine, the last of his energy draining out of him. It had been a long and stressful day. Between worrying about meeting Brooklyn and Gayle and now all this, it was a wonder he was still functioning at all.

"Okay. We'll keep digging and see if we can come up with anything new. You go home and get some rest and let us know immediately if you think of anything else. No matter how insignificant you may think it is, we want to hear it." He handed me his business card.

I looked it over, noting both his work and cell number on there then shoved it in my pocket.

"Do you think it's safe for him to go home? Maybe I should take him to a hotel or something," I suggested.

Oliver looked at me and shook his head. "I really just want to be in my own bed tonight, please."

Detective Rogers looked over at his partner who must have read his mind because he was already standing and heading for the door. "On it," he called out over his shoulder.

"We'll have a couple of our guys stationed outside your apartment. Anybody tries to get inside and they'll stop them." Oliver nodded tiredly, and I helped him to his feet, holding onto him when he swayed a bit. "Thank you for coming in and for all your help. We're going to get this guy," he said firmly.

I shook his hand and promised again that we'd call if we were able to think of anything. Oliver was silent the entire way home, his head facing away from me as he stared out the passenger window. I'd be surprised if he even noticed anything that was out there though. It broke my heart to see him hurting so badly.

Meanwhile, I was trying very hard not to let my horror show over the fact that a serial killer had his sights set on the man that I loved. I'd spent the first thirty-seven years of my life not knowing what it meant to be in love, but that all changed the moment I met Oliver.

I'd been fortunate enough to have love in my life. My parents loved me, despite our tendency to butt heads. Gayle and I loved each other in the protective and caring way that best friends do. I would lay down my life for Brooklyn, but I'd always known that eventually, I'd have to let her go. Oliver was the only person in my life who made my heart beat faster every time he walked in the room and whose absence could be felt like a physical presence.

I was completely, passionately, and beyond any sense of reason, in love with the man beside me. My life had become infinitely better the moment he entered it and I never wanted to let that go. I never wanted to lose him. Especially not to a madman.

It was after midnight by the time we got home. I parked in front of Oliver's apartment and turned off the car. My eyes scanned the area, paying close attention to the shadowed corners of the building in case a monster was lurking there. I'd never felt so aware of my surroundings as I did right then.

"Do you think it's my fault?" My head whipped over to Oliver. It was the first time he'd spoken since leaving the station and I cringed as I heard the dull, detached tone of his voice. It sounded all wrong coming from a man who was always so full of energy and sass.

"Do I think what's your fault, baby?"

I watched him swallow. "Is it my fault they're all dead? All those guys whose pictures were hanging on the wall? Korey?" A sob tore from his chest and his face crumpled as he began to cry.

I undid his seatbelt and then pulled him into my arms, as much as the armrest would allow. It was uncomfortable, and I wasn't anywhere near as close to him as I wanted to be, but I'd be damned if I was going to allow him to blame himself for what that sick bastard had done.

"You listen to me. You are not to blame for any of this. Whoever is doing this is sick and evil and he alone is responsible for those men's deaths. He decided to commit these unspeakable crimes, not you. So, I don't want to hear another word about this being your fault because it's just not true, okay?" He nodded, but I could tell he still wasn't convinced. I sighed. I knew it was going to take some time, but I'd spend each and every day repeating those words if that's what it would take for him to finally believe me.

I climbed from the car and went around to open his door. There was a black SUV parked nearby and I spotted two men inside. My heart pounded loudly in my ears, but then one of them gave a subtle nod and I realized they must be the undercover police officers Detective Rogers had sent over.

I felt better knowing they were there, but only marginally. If it were up to me, I'd have the entire L.A.P.D. camping outside his door. I made a mental note to hire a private security detail first thing in the morning. When it came to the safety of the man I loved, I wasn't taking any chances.

I got Oliver inside and he waited quietly as I went around and made sure all the doors and windows were locked. I followed him down the hallway toward his room, but he turned and stepped into the bathroom instead. I leaned my shoulder against the doorway as he started the shower. I probably should've given him some privacy and I would've given it to him if he'd asked for it, but until he did, I just couldn't force myself to let him out of my sight.

I watched as he pulled his designer suit jacket off and let it drop to the floor, too tired to care what happened to it. The rest of his clothes followed and then he looked over at me and held his hand out. I was standing in front of him a second later, removing my own clothes and tossing them on the floor. My arms went around him the second we were in the shower and he buried his face in my neck, his cries ringing out, louder than the sound of the water spraying down over our bodies.

I held him in my arms, gently rocking him back and forth as he cried for those men and for Korey who despite his betrayal, deserved better than to be brutally murdered and discarded in some dumpster like day-old garbage. Tears flowed silently down my own cheeks, the evidence of them quickly washed away by the shower. I cried for Oliver and what this had already done to him, how this would affect him in the future and for the utter helplessness I felt.

I washed him gently and then quickly washed myself before stepping out and drying us both off. I helped him into bed and turned off the light before crawling in beside him. "I need you," Oliver whispered in the dark.

"I'm right here, baby," I answered, pulling him toward me.

"No. I *need* you," he reemphasized.

"Are you sure? I can just hold..."

"Please, Samuel. I feel empty right now. Like all the evilness has stolen everything good that used to be there. I need to feel your warmth and your love. I need you over me and inside of me until all I can feel, all I can think about is *you*."

He didn't need to ask again, because there was nothing I wouldn't give, wouldn't do for this man. Plus, I needed it just as badly as he did. I needed to make love with him, to feel his heart beating against mine and to wipe out the fear that he was going to disappear somehow.

I reached into the bedside table and pulled out the supplies before rolling back toward him. We didn't bother with foreplay, neither of us had the patience for that right then. We kissed as I carefully prepared his body to take me. We were both trembling with need as I quickly slid the condom onto my cock, slicked it and lined it up against him.

A sob tore from his chest as I broke through the tight ring of muscle, and I froze, afraid that I'd hurt him in some way. "Don't stop. Oh, God, Samuel, please don't stop," he cried desperately.

With a possessive growl, I slid the rest of the way until I was as deep inside him as I could go. Tears sprang to my eyes over the feel of his warmth and vitality. I'd needed this, a reminder that he was still there, safe and whole in my arms. His arms and legs wrapped around me and he held me close as I rocked into him. Everything else about the day began to fade as I got lost in the sensations of his body around my cock, his arms around my shoulders and his lips pressed to mine.

Our movements sped up, the two of us perfectly in sync with each other as we raced toward a release that would free us from all the pain and the ugliness, if only for a few seconds. Oliver went soaring first, throwing his head back on the pillow and shouting my name as hot liquid spilled between us. His body continued convulsing as he rode the waves of pleasure and the tightening of his inner walls around my cock was enough to send me over the edge too.

Careful not to crush him, I collapsed beside him on the bed. I was still trying to catch my breath as he removed the condom from my spent cock and disposed of it then he curled up into my side, laying soft kisses along the side of my neck.

"I love you," I whispered. There was no answer though because exhaustion had claimed him, his lips still pressed against my skin.

A sound startled me awake. The room was mostly dark, only a tiny bit of light shining through the window. Oliver was still snoring softly next to me, the peaceful sound soothing to my ears. *Probably just one of the neighbors getting home late.* A glance at the clock showed that we'd only been asleep an hour, so I rolled over on my side and tried to settle back to sleep.

Another noise had my eyes popping open and ice water running through my veins, mostly because it had come from inside the bedroom. Heart racing, I rolled toward Oliver to warn him, but before I got the chance, something solid and heavy slammed into the back of my head. Pain exploded behind my eyes and a wave of dizziness like I'd never experienced before had me falling back against the pillow.

From behind the blanket of pain, I heard more noises and the sounds of a struggle. I leaned up, desperate to get to Oliver, but something slammed into my jaw, leaving me careening over the side of the bed. My head smacked hard against the side table and the last thing I remembered before I lost consciousness was the sound of Oliver's muffled cries.

NINETEEN

Oliver

My head was pounding, and my throat felt scratchy and dry. Even though I'd just woken, I felt like I hadn't slept in days. *What's wrong with me? Am I getting sick?* Maybe Samuel would get me some medicine or a cool drink to soothe my throat. I lifted my head to ask him, but a wave of dizziness crashed into me and I quickly lay back down.

I heard a clicking noise, somewhere off in the distance. Something about it was familiar, but my mind was too muddled to make sense of it. As I lay there, it continued. A click right next to my ear made me flinch, but just as quickly, it was gone. With no discernible rhythm, it seemed to be moving in all directions, its volume increasing, only to decrease a few seconds later.

As my head began to clear, bits and pieces of memories started to filter through. Samuel looking handsome and distinguished in his suit as he introduced me to Brooklyn as *his Oliver*, the police, morbid pictures of young men, Korey…dead. Not just dead but murdered. Holding Samuel as he made love to me and then a noise… something soft, covering my nose and mouth and a sickly-sweet smell as I breathed in.

Gasping, my eyes sprang open as I suddenly remembered, but I recoiled immediately as a blinding white light pierced my eyes. I screwed them tightly shut as the pain in my head came back with a vengeance, stealing my breath and causing my stomach to revolt. I took several deep breaths through my nose, releasing them slowly through pursed lips until the pain had dulled and I no longer felt like I was going to throw up.

Vowing not to make the same mistake twice, I slowly began to open my eyes, allowing them to adjust to the light a little at a time. When they were finally opened all the way, I sat up. A cold chill swept over me and I shivered. Looking down, I saw I was wearing my pink, silk robe and a quick peek inside told me I was naked underneath. My stomach roiled again at the thought of someone touching me while I'd lain unconscious and vulnerable.

Holding my breath, I squirmed around a bit, testing for any soreness that would tell me I'd been violated. My relief was so great when I felt none that I swayed and nearly fell back on the bed, but then I remembered that I was alone for the moment and whoever had brought me there could be back at any second. I had to try and figure out where I was and search for anything that could possibly be used as a weapon. I needed to protect myself and I needed to hurry.

I was sitting in the middle of a bed in what appeared to be someone's home. But instead of separate rooms, it was just one big, open space. Something about it seemed vaguely familiar, but I was certain I'd never been in that particular place before.

A kitchen area took up the entire wall, opposite from me and a moveable divider separated what I guessed to be a bathroom from the rest of the room. A small seating area with a futon and two overstuffed chairs, sat along a wall containing three large windows with the shades drawn. Through them, I was able to determine that it was still dark outside, and the sounds out there made me think I might be in the city, rather than some remote location. That was good. Cities meant people and people meant help. I just had to figure out how to get to them.

My eyes scanned the room again, but there were no framed photos or personal items lying about which might offer a clue as to whose home I was in. In fact, the only thing I recognized at all was the light which had hurt my eyes because I'd seen others like it plenty of times before, just never in someone's bedroom.

Moving as quickly as I could, I tossed my feet over the side of the bed and stood on wobbly legs. It was already too late though. The sound of footsteps approaching had me looking across the room as the door swung open and a man stepped inside. My jaw dropped open as my mind scrambled to come up with a logical reason for why he'd be there.

"Ah! You're awake. Good." He smiled at me and a sense of dread settled in the pit of my stomach while a part of me still hoped I was wrong.

"What's going on? Where am I and why am I here, Ben?" I whispered. He shrugged and for the first time, I noticed the camera he was holding. Suddenly, the trifold floor lamp and the clicking sound I'd heard earlier started to make sense. *Had he been taking my picture while I'd been passed out?*

"I'd hoped it would be obvious," he said.

"It's been a really long day for me, perhaps you should spell it out," I said through clenched teeth. I could feel panic starting to set in and I fought to keep it at bay. If I was going to figure a way out of this, I would have to keep my wits about me.

"You're in my home above the studio. I brought you here because you belong with me." I stared at him, waiting for the punchline, but his face remained serious.

Apparently, the joke had been on me. How could I have been so close to two people, yet never known what they were truly like? First, I'd found out Korey was stealing from me and now Ben, who I'd also thought was my friend and a decent guy had…kidnapped me? What the hell was really going on? His words to me when we'd talked about Korey made a lot more sense now. He'd told me that people only let you see the parts of themselves they want you to see. Had he been referring to himself as well as Korey?

I shivered as it felt like an icy-cold finger traced a line down my spine. Was Ben the serial killer or was this something else altogether? I was praying for the latter, even though it wouldn't mean I was in any less danger. Still, if he was the serial killer, then that would mean…

"Did you kill Korey?" I'd spoken the words so quietly that I wasn't sure he'd heard, but he smiled and took a step toward me. Instinctively, I took a step back but stopped short as my knees hit the edge of the bed.

He continued advancing until he was right in front of me, barely a breath between us. "Yes. And I did it all for you." The calm, concise manner in which he said it, had me breaking out in a cold sweat and I started to shake as the acrid smell of my own fear singed my nostrils.

Even after his admission, my mind tried to reject the idea. It was impossible to marry the two Bens together in my mind. The Ben I'd always known had been playful, fun and creative. The one standing in front of me was a total stranger, with eyes that held a cold detachment as he told me that he'd murdered someone. How could I have spent so many hours with someone and never been able to see how completely psychotic he was? Was I really that naïve or was Ben just a master at hiding it?

"What do you mean you did it all for me?" I asked in a shaky voice.

"The guy was always a complete asshole. You trusted him, but he never deserved your trust; I did. I could tell for a long time that he was up to no good, but you kept right on believing him. I was so glad when you finally figured out that he was stealing from you, but I felt bad that you were hurting. So, I took care of the situation.

Korey Duncan was nothing but trash...so that's where he ended up." A manic laugh bubbled up from his throat, making him sound even more deranged than he already obviously was.

"What about all those other guys? Did you kill them too?" I whispered, not wanting to hear the answer, but finding it necessary at the same time. I needed to understand, to try and make sense of what was going on.

Ben set his camera down on the side table then reached a hand up to touch my face, but I recoiled. His eyes narrowed, and something dark and sinister flashed in his eyes, then just as quickly it was gone, replaced with a strange, almost wolfish grin. "That's okay, my love. You'll be begging for my touch soon enough." I tasted bile in the back of my throat at the thought of him touching me. Did he really think I'd ever let him touch me after the things he'd done? If so, he was even crazier than I thought.

He took a step back and I blew out a relieved breath. That was, until he answered my question. "Yes, I killed them too. Every single one of them. I felt bad doing it, some of them were quite beautiful, but they were there to serve a purpose."

"What purpose?" I wrapped my arms around myself to try and control my shaking.

He looked at me like the answer should've been obvious. "To keep me from killing you, of course."

"Why would you want to kill me? I thought we were friends," I choked out as tears filled my eyes. I used the back of my hand to brush them away.

"That's the thing. I didn't *want* to kill you. I love you. But sometimes the...voice would tell me to kill you; that you were just like all the others who'd rejected me or snubbed their noses at me because I was *just the photographer*. They liked me well enough while I was snapping their pictures, but then they moved on to people who could help them get further along in their careers. People like Korey." He was becoming increasingly agitated the more he spoke, and I needed to diffuse the situation before he lost it completely and decided to listen to the voice in his head.

"I thought you were straight," I said lamely. I knew in the grand scope of things, that information held little significance, but it was the first thing that popped in my head.

Ben threw his head back and laughed and I breathed a sigh of relief that it had worked. "Why would you think that?"

"Because I saw you kissing a woman. The first time we worked together, she was leaving your studio," I said weakly.

Coming closer, Ben reached for me again, but he refused to let me back away that time. His hands clamped down on either side of my face, holding me in place. Despite his firm grip, he tilted his head and smiled like he thought I was precious. "Sweetie, I'm bisexual. You of all people should've considered that as a possibility. Especially given your little fuck buddy." His upper lip curled back into a sneer when he mentioned Samuel and his hold tightened around my face, fingers digging in painfully and I whimpered.

Hearing the sound seemed to snap him out of whatever place he'd gone in his head and he let go. Thinking of Samuel brought a different kind of pain to my chest. I remember him trying to fight Ben off, to keep him from getting to me. Then Ben had hit him, and he'd disappeared over the side of the bed. Was he hurt? He was probably going out of his mind trying to find me, just as I would be if he'd been the one who was taken.

I had to get back to Samuel, but first, I'd have to figure a way out of there. I needed to keep him talking. "I know you were upset about what Korey did to me, but you two never got along. Was there some sort of history there?"

Ben let out a long sigh, then turned and headed over to the windows. Pulling one of the shades up, he leaned his shoulder against the frame and stared out at the city. "You're right. There was a history there and it wasn't a good one."

"What happened?" I asked, darting my eyes to the door. Ben

hadn't locked it when he'd come through.

"When I was a kid, I was bounced around from one foster home to the next. My parents didn't want me, so I became a ward of the state. Every home was the same. They'd start out all nice, but eventually they'd start to realize I wasn't as strong or as smart or as good at sports as the other kids there and they'd come up with some excuse to get rid of me. In high school, I never fit in. Guys beat me up for liking other guys and girls avoided me because they couldn't understand what was wrong with me. Hell, I didn't understand it myself. I'd been looked down on my entire life, never quite living up to anyone's expectations of me."

Listening to his story with one ear, I took a tentative step toward the door. Just one, and then I paused, waiting to see if he'd catch me. My shoulders sagged in relief as he continued his story. "I'd always liked taking pictures. I got my first camera when I was twelve. Some skinny guy dressed up as Santa showed up at the foster home I was at with gifts for all us kids. I overheard him and my foster mom talking and he said he was from one of the local churches and bringing us stuff was part of their charity outreach. I didn't care though. It was the first present I'd ever gotten."

Keeping my eyes on him, I managed another two steps, then stopped to calculate the distance and how far I should try to sneak before making a run for it. I was pretty quick, but I had no idea how fast Ben was and I'd never had to run for my life before.

"I loved taking pictures. There was something peaceful about seeing the world through a tiny viewfinder that made it seem more manageable, less daunting. It helped calm the voices inside my head."

"You heard the voices even then?" I asked without thinking. He glanced at me over his shoulder and I cursed my stupidity in drawing attention to myself. I held my breath, hoping he wouldn't notice that I'd moved.

"I don't like to talk about that," he said firmly. I nodded my head; thankful I hadn't been caught. He turned his head back to the set of windows. I was thankful that he'd left the shades drawn on the other windows or he would've been able to see my reflection and my escape attempt wouldn't have been possible.

"Anyway, I got a job and paid my way through college, earning my Bachelor of Arts in Photography. A magazine saw my work and hired me. My career grew from there, making one connection after another until I was able to open my own studio and work independently. For the first time in my life, people weren't looking down on me. They liked my work and they respected me. Then I met Julian."

"Who's Julian?" I asked. I'd only shuffled a few more steps, but it was enough that if he turned around, he'd be able to tell I'd moved.

"Julian was a model that came to me to have some headshots taken. He showed up at my studio with his agent, Korey." I froze, mid-step as he mentioned Korey's name. "He was fairly new to the business, but I could tell right away he'd go far. He was stunning, with smooth, flawless skin, a lithe body, and gorgeous blond hair. We worked together several times and I slowly got to know him. We became friends and I decided to take a chance and ask him out."

I was happy with the progress I'd made, but I still was only halfway to the door. I needed to go further, but I was reaching that point where if I wasn't careful, Ben might see me in his periphery. My heart was pounding so hard, I was sure he was going to hear it.

Ben's voice sounded colder this time. "I shouldn't have been surprised when he turned me down. Said he just saw me as a friend, nothing more. Of course, Korey walked in right then and overheard him rejecting me. I was humiliated, and Korey knew it. He made sure to pull me aside after Julian had left and remind me that I would never be good enough for someone like Julian.

"Something inside me snapped that day and the voice which had always been more of a whisper, suddenly began screaming at me. It told me that Korey was right. I would never be accepted because I would never be good enough. I took all the hurt and rage that I'd kept bottled up for years and unleashed it later that night in Julian's apartment. He looked so scared and he stared at me the whole time like he didn't understand what was happening. I choked him so hard, I nearly severed his spinal cord."

I covered my mouth to stifle a sob as I pictured the terror the young man had to have experienced in his final moments. I couldn't let the same thing happen to me. I fought back against the panic that threatened to take over and forced myself to focus on getting out of there. All I needed to do was make it outside and I'd run screaming until I woke the whole neighborhood up and somebody either helped me or called the police.

"Julian was my first," Ben said reverently. It was clear that he was lost in the memory, so I took the opportunity to scoot closer to the door. Ben chuckled. "I was so nervous those next few weeks as I wondered if the police would show up at my door. I took to stalking his friends, so I could hear what was being said about his disappearance. But, as it turned out, I didn't need to worry. Korey, being such an asshole, had been making Julian's life miserable to the point that he'd been talking to his friends about quitting and moving to New York to pursue acting instead. When he disappeared, they just assumed that's where he'd gone. Korey tried to cause a fuss, but they told him it was his own damn fault. No one ever did find his body," Ben boasted. I thought I was going to throw up from the pride in his voice.

"The first time you walked in was like a punch to the gut. You looked so much like Julian, except his eyes were blue and he had long hair. The voice told me that I shouldn't take any chances, that I should kill you before you had the chance to reject me the way Julian had." My jaw dropped as he spoke about killing me as easily as if he were discussing the weather.

"Julian had always been friendly, but we never really talked about anything other than work. That very first day, I mentioned something about a shoot I'd done in Australia. You started firing off all these questions, wanting to know about the food, the weather, what my favorite thing was about the country. You were the very first person who'd shown a genuine interest in me beyond my photos. I knew then that you were going to be different, but I was still cautious, so I decided to wait and see.

"Each time I worked with you was more of the same. Even when Korey was being at his worst, you were always nice to me and wanted to talk. I felt myself falling for you, but the voice inside my head kept getting louder, telling me to get rid of you before you hurt me. I didn't want to do that though. I wasn't ready to let you go yet."

I knew I should keep moving, but suddenly I found it impossible to move as I listened to him. I'd had no idea how close I'd come to death. One wrong move on my part, one sharply spoken word and he could've given in to the voice's command and killed me. How easily could it have been my picture up on that wall at the police station. I might never have had the chance to meet Samuel. That last thought had tears swimming in my eyes and it took everything in my power not to give in to my despair. By whatever grace there was, I had stayed on good terms with Ben and I had met Samuel and I was going to fight like hell to get back to him.

"One night, I was out at a club. It had been a shit day and I was there to get drunk. There was this guy there; blond, skinny, cute. I was watching him grind up on some guy on the dance floor and then it happened. The voice started in, trying to convince me that it was you and you were just trying to make a fool of me by dancing with that other guy. I met him on his way out to his car that night and choked him behind the dumpster. I knew in the back of my mind that he wasn't you but killing him appeased the voice. I was in love with you by then and I'd already decided I wasn't going to let you go. I just needed to kill guys that looked like you instead. It was the only way to quiet the voice, but still keep you."

Ben turned around then, the look on his face pleading with me to understand. Confusion swept over his features though when I wasn't standing where he'd expected me to be. Knowing I only had seconds, I took off running. I'd managed to close the gap between me and the door until there were only a few feet left and I tore across the floor, literally running for my life.

Adrenaline surged through my veins as I raced to the bottom of the steps and flung the door open to his studio. The pounding of footsteps behind me told me Ben was right on my heels, but I didn't dare look back, it would only slow me down. I sprinted across the studio and reached for the doorknob, screaming at the top of my lungs.

I was still running as I felt myself being lifted in the air. Before I could make sense of what was happening, I was tossed to the ground, my head cracking loudly against the unforgiving hardwood floor. Ben was on top of me a second later, his heavier bulk landing on me with a thud. The air whooshed out of my lungs and I barely had time to draw a breath in when his hands landed on my neck, his fingers circling my throat.

I tried to buck him off of me, twisting and turning underneath him in a desperate attempt to dislodge the hold he had on me, but it seemed to only enrage him more. His thumbs dug into the hollow of my throat and I reached up, clawing at his eyes and leaving bloody scratches down his cheeks.

"You were supposed to be different!" Ben roared above me. Staring up at him, his face purple with rage and his eyes wild with bloodthirst, I knew I was staring at the face of the Devil himself.

My vision began to darken around the edges and I could feel my arms going slack as my energy seeped out of me. I knew I only had seconds left, and while that should've terrified me, I felt a sense of peace instead. I'd always heard people say that your life flashes before your eyes right before you die, but I'd never been sure what they meant, until that moment. Turns out, it isn't your whole life, so much as all the very best moments from your life. At least for me it was.

Playing like scenes from a movie, I saw images of the very first time I saw Samuel and his blue eyes connected with mine. The way he blushed whenever I flirted with him, the deep baritone of his laugh and the way his lips felt when pressed against mine. The sparkle in his eyes when he was excited and the gentle look he'd get whenever I told him I loved him. The feel of him inside me, his arms wrapped around me as he whispered words of love in my ear.

The images never stopped. They continued, one after the other, bringing me a feeling of comfort and love as the last bit of light faded away.

TWENTY

Samuel

I grunted as I sat up, confused about how I'd wound up on the floor instead of in the bed. My head pounded, and I reached up, wincing as I touched the spot where it felt like someone had taken a sledgehammer to the back of my skull. There was a large knot there and when I pulled away, my hand was coated with a wet, sticky substance. *What the hell was going on?* A wave of nausea made my stomach roll, but one look at the other side of the bed had me leaping to my feet, the pain in my head forgotten.

I flicked on the lamp beside the bed, wincing at the sudden brightness. Oliver's side of the bed was a mess. Blanket and sheets twisted around each other, pillow near the foot of the bed and the fitted sheet pulled off the corner of the bed, exposing the bare mattress beneath. Everything that had happened came rushing back, the horror of it all slamming into me like a punch to the gut. Someone had been in the apartment. They'd hit me and then gone for Oliver. I'd tried to get to Oliver, to stop the person from hurting him, but then a fist had knocked me backward.

Icy-cold fingers trailed down my spine and I took off running through the apartment, calling out for him. Terror seized me as I realized he was gone and I bent over at the waist, leaning my hands on my knees as I tried to fight back my panic. I could fall apart later, but right then, Oliver needed me, and every single second counted.

I sprinted to the bathroom and grabbed my wrinkled suit up off the floor then ran back to the bedroom, pulling the business card out of the back pocket of my pants. Detective Rogers answered on the second ring and I hit speaker before setting the phone on the bed.

"He's gone!" I shouted. "Somebody came into the apartment. They knocked me out and when I woke up, Oliver was gone." I raced around the room, pulling my clothes on. My hands were shaking so badly, it took me three tries before I finally managed to get my shirt buttoned.

"How long ago?" Detective Rogers' voice was calm and precise, but it did nothing to quell the fear that had been squeezing my heart from the moment I realized Oliver had been taken.

"I don't know. Maybe five, ten minutes at most?" I told him.

"Okay, I'm going to get every available officer from the L.A.P.D. on this. You sit tight, and I'll let you know as soon as I hear something."

"You have to find him. Please, Detective Rogers. I can't lose him. I can't…" My voice broke at the end and I covered my mouth with the back of my hand to hold in a sob.

I heard him sigh through the phone. "We'll comb this entire city until we find him. I promise, Samuel. We're going to stop this bastard once and for all." It was impossible to speak around the lump in my throat, but I didn't have to. He'd already hung up anyway.

I tossed my phone aside and sank down onto the bed, tears welling up in my eyes. I'd never felt so afraid or more helpless in my entire life. The man I loved with every fiber of my being was missing; taken by some monster who for whatever reason had become fixated on him and had killed before. The idea that I may never see Oliver, never get to hold him in my arms or hear his laugh ever again had me doubling over.

I wrapped my arms around my middle, trying to hold myself together as the fear and the pain threatened to tear me apart. *How am I supposed to do this? How am I supposed to just sit here alone while Oliver is out there somewhere?* Picking my phone back up, I called the only person I could think of who could help me right then.

"Please, I need you," I whispered brokenly.

"I'm on my way. Tell me what's going on," Gayle said. I could hear the phone rustling as she moved around and then quiet murmuring as she spoke to someone on her end.

My shoulders sagged wearily as I told her everything that had happened since we'd left the restaurant after having dinner with them. Had it really only been a few hours since we'd all been together? It seemed like an entire lifetime had passed since that one perfect moment. I'd felt so happy, so complete and I'd thought that my life couldn't possibly get any better. Then, within hours, everything had shattered, and Oliver's life was left hanging in the balance.

Gayle promised she'd be there as quickly as possible and we hung up. A few seconds later, there was a knock at the front door. Leaping to my feet, I rushed to answer it, hoping it would be Detective Rogers bringing Oliver back to me. My heart sank though when the two men in the doorway held up their badges. I recognized them right away as the two undercover cops who'd been sent to guard the place and all of my anguish turned into a furious anger in the blink of an eye.

"Where the hell were you guys? You were supposed to make sure no one got in here. You were supposed to keep him safe," I shouted.

One of the officers held his hands up in a placating gesture. "Sir, we understand you're upset, but we can assure you, we were watching the front of the building the entire time. We would've seen if anyone had gone in or out of here."

"With your permission, we'd like to have a look around just in case this guy might have left something behind that might give us a clue who he is or where to find him," the taller of the two men said.

My anger drained out of me as quickly as it had risen. There was no point hanging onto it when that energy could be better spent trying to do something to help Oliver. Stepping aside, I gestured for them to come inside. I showed them back to the bedroom and went over everything once again as they searched under the bed, around the floor and in each room.

"Pretty sure this is how he got in here," the taller officer called from down the hall. I followed the sound of his voice and found him next to the open back door. Looks like he jimmied the lock with something sharp, possibly a screwdriver because the wood's been split around it. Also, this door faces the rear of the building which would explain how he could get in here and carry Mr. Hughes back out without us seeing," he explained.

My hands went to my hips and I tilted my head back, taking deep breaths through my nose as another wave of nausea hit. How long had he been in there? Did he come in after we fell asleep or had he been there while we were making love? My imagination went wild, picturing every scenario, each one more horrifying than the first.

Another knock at the door saved me from torturing myself any further and I rushed to go answer it. This time when I opened it, I saw the worried, loving faces of my family. Gayle, Brooklyn, and even Andrew all rushed forward to wrap their arms around me and for the first time since I'd woken up, I allowed myself to fall apart.

Andrew set to work making a pot of coffee while Gayle got a wet washcloth. Her fingers were gentle as she started cleaning the area around my wound, looking it over and proclaiming in her firm, mothering voice that I should be checked for a concussion. I was too tired to argue with her, so I just nodded, but that was going to have to wait, I needed to find Oliver first.

Brooklyn sat next to me on the couch and held my hand,

quietly assuring me that Oliver was going to be alright. I tried to cling to her optimism, but the sinking feeling in my chest, prevented me from fully believing it. The officers came out awhile later and said that they hadn't been able to find anything else, so they were going to help with the search. I nodded numbly as they left, staring at the door as it shut behind them.

"Okay, let's go," Gayle said after they'd been gone a minute. I turned and gave her a puzzled look. "I mean it. We're only going to make ourselves nuts if we sit here. Oliver needs us, and you need to feel like you're doing something. Let's get in the car and go look for him." The look on her face showed that she was absolutely serious, and I couldn't remember ever being more grateful to have her by my side.

The four of us packed into Andrew's car and set off to comb the streets looking for Oliver. Tirelessly, we drove around, stopping to ask anyone we happened to see out walking if they'd seen Oliver and showing them a picture of him from my phone.

My heart felt heavy each time they shook their heads no, but Brooklyn, Gayle, and Andrew would be ready with some encouraging words and we'd take off again until we found another person to ask. I'd lost track of how many streets we'd driven and the number of people we'd asked when suddenly, my phone rang, startling us all. My heart stuttered when I saw it was Detective Rogers' number on the screen.

"Hello." My hands felt clammy and my pulse raced as I answered.

"Samuel, we were able to locate Oliver." I sagged in my seat and let out a long breath, but then I noticed the tentative tone in his voice.

"Where is he? Is he okay?" I asked nervously.

"You need to get to the hospital right away. I'll meet you and explain everything there." The hesitant way he spoke told me that things weren't good, and I dropped my phone.

In the distance, I saw Gayle grab my phone and put it to her ear, listening to the detective and asking which hospital we should go to. But it was as if I were listening from underwater. The voices around me became muffled as my mind tried to shut down in order to protect itself.

"Daddy, we're here," Brooklyn said softly.

I shook the fog from my mind and looked around, surprised to see that we'd already arrived at the hospital. My door was open, and she was standing in front of it, waiting for me to step out. I wasn't sure how long they'd been trying to get my attention, but it must have been long enough to worry them because they both were looking at me with concern.

My face flushed as I turned and got out of the car and started walking toward the emergency room entrance. Part of me wanted to run through those doors and demand answers and the other part of me wanted to get back in the car and drive far away from whatever truths had made the detective sound like that.

What would I do if I got in there and they told me Oliver was gone? That I'd lost him for good? My heart and my head were in complete agreement, refusing to allow me to even picture that scenario. As if she'd heard my thoughts and knew how fragile I was at the moment, Brooklyn reached for me. She took my hand and squeezed it firmly in hers, lending me her strength. I gave her a grateful, watery smile.

The automatic doors swooshed open and the four of us stepped inside. Detective Rogers was speaking to the nurse at the front desk, but when he saw me, he rushed over. His face was tired and worn and he looked like he'd aged ten years since I'd first met him at the station. I was sure I wasn't fairing much better though. After some quick introductions to the rest of my family, he led us back to a private room where we could talk. My hands were ice cold as he sat down across from me and looked me in the eyes.

"After I got your call saying that Oliver was missing, Detective

Billings and I ran through the list of names Oliver had given us of people he worked with that didn't like Korey. We felt like that would be the most logical place to start since they would have ties with both Oliver and Korey. I sent officers out to each address we had, both work and residential. I wasn't going to leave anything to chance. Not long after they were sent out, I got a call from dispatch. A man had called in to report someone screaming in the building next door. Dispatch immediately recognized the address as one of the places I had just sent the officers out to investigate and wanted to warn me of a possible violent situation in progress. The address they gave was for a photography studio with a residence above. The owner was Benjamin Turner."

"Ben?" I whispered. My head spun, trying to wrap my mind around what the detective had just told me. I'd never met the man, but Oliver had always spoken so highly of his work and about him as a friend. Was he the one behind all of the killings and Korey's murder? Was he the one who took Oliver? My heart shattered, and tears welled up in my eyes as I pictured Oliver, learning that he'd been betrayed yet again by someone he'd thought was his friend, someone he'd trusted. My poor baby.

"Detective Billings and I arrived at the scene just moments behind the other officers. They'd busted through the door when they saw the two men inside. Ben was on top of Oliver and he was choking him. Oliver wasn't moving." I could hear Brooklyn start to cry next to me, but I kept staring at the detective, willing him to finish his story. I needed to know.

"A couple of officers tackled Ben, knocking him off of Oliver. He fought back and somehow in the scuffle, Ben got ahold of a gun." I could feel sweat trickle down the side of my face despite feeling cold everywhere else. "Ben turned the gun on Oliver and the officers who were performing CPR on him. He was a direct threat to everyone in that room, so he had to be taken down. Officers fired several shots and Ben was killed."

"What about Oliver? Is he going to be okay?" I asked, fear making my voice shake. Detective Rogers looked down at his feet and my hands gripped the arms of the chair, bracing myself for his next words. When he looked back up, his eyes were haunted.

"He died at the scene." Gayle gasped on the other side of me and I felt the blood drain out of my face, but Detective Rogers held his hands up. "EMTs got there and they were able to revive him, but he was in very bad shape when he got here. He's back with the doctors now. They'll check him out and then come talk to us." My heart restarted itself. Oliver was alive. I repeated those words over and over in my head, trying to convince myself that they were true.

There was a knock on the door and we all turned to look as a doctor peeked his head inside. "Excuse me, I'm looking for Detective Rogers," he said.

"That's me." The detective stood and shook the doctor's hand as he stepped into the room.

"I'm Doctor Hammond. I wanted to discuss my findings with the patient connected to your case." His eyes moved over the rest of us cautiously, as if he wasn't sure what he could say just yet.

"You can speak freely in here, Doctor Hammond. This is Samuel Bishop and his family. Samuel is Oliver's boyfriend. Anything you need to discuss concerning Oliver Hughes can be said to him," Detective Rogers informed him. I gave him a grateful look.

"Okay then, let's sit down and I'll go over everything," Doctor Hammond said. The two of them took seats across from us and the doctor gave me a gentle smile. "I'm assuming Detective Rogers has already updated you on the severity of Oliver's situation." I nodded, swallowing around the lump in my throat.

"He suffered multiple bruises, but the worst damage is of course, to his neck. He has torn tissue inside and out and deep bruising to the larynx. Many of the blood vessels in his neck and face burst, making him appear much worse than his condition actually is. He needs to refrain from talking as much as possible over the next few days. I also want to keep him for twenty-four hours, so we can observe him and make sure no other issues arise. All in all, I'd have to say that Oliver is one very lucky man." We all shared a collective sigh of relief and Gayle and Brooklyn took turns hugging me. I couldn't wipe the smile off my face and I noticed that Detective Rogers seemed to be suffering from the same affliction.

"When can I see him, Doctor?" I asked anxiously. I needed to see Oliver like I needed my next breath.

"I'll walk you to his room."

After hugging Gayle and Brooklyn and shaking hands with Andrew, I sent them home to get some rest. They wanted to see Oliver too, but understood that I needed some time alone with him, so they promised to come back after a few hours. I shook Detective Rogers' hand and thanked him for everything he had done to find Oliver then I followed the doctor to Oliver's room.

He looked so small and fragile lying in that hospital bed, the sound of machines beeping all around him and I gasped when I saw the angry purple and red bruising around his eyes and throat. Tears were streamed down my face as I pulled up a chair alongside his bed and took his hand. He didn't stir so I lowered my head to our hands and sobbed, saying a prayer of thanks that he hadn't been taken from me.

Oliver's fingers tightened around my hand and I lifted my head. The most beautiful pair of chestnut-colored eyes were staring back at me. They were full of fear and sadness, but they also held love. He opened his mouth to say something, but I held my hand up to stop him.

"The doctor said you're not allowed to talk." His chin quivered so I carefully climbed on the bed and wrapped my arms around him. "You don't need to say anything though, baby. I know, I know."

I held him then as we cried together, sharing our pain, and our fear and finding relief in the safety of each other's arms. I had the man I loved back with me and I was never going to let him go again. I could handle anything that came my way as long as he was by my side.

EPILOGUE

Samuel

One year later

I
t had been a full year since that terrible night when I thought
I'd lost him. The physical wounds had healed rather quickly for
Oliver, but the emotional scars left behind required a lot more
work. He began seeing a therapist who was helping him work
through his feelings of betrayal by both Ben and Korey along with
the guilt he felt over Ben's victims. It had taken a long time, but
he had slowly begun to accept that he was not responsible for their
deaths.

Trust had become a very difficult thing for Oliver. Not only did
he have trouble trusting others, but he also struggled with trusting
his own instincts after being proven so very wrong about both men.
Even though he swore that he trusted me implicitly, his therapist
had urged us to attend couples counseling to deal with any trust
issues that may arise as well as the trauma we'd been through the
night Oliver was taken.

Looking at him now, it was amazing to think that he was the
same man who had been so broken and torn when he'd left the

hospital a year ago. After months of depression and nightmares, Oliver had slowly begun to come back to me. I cried the first time I saw him smile again and we'd wept together as we made love. There were still bad days, for both of us, but for the most part, he was back to being the fun-loving, sassy man I'd fallen in love with. He was back to being *my Oliver*.

As with any major change or event in a person's life, we each had taken inventory of our lives, deciding what was most important to us as individuals and as a couple. Oliver continued to model for the time being but decided to pursue his love of fashion and had enrolled in design school. Refusing to let me pay off the debt Korey had created, he still worked a few runway shows and was using that money to pay off the credit cards. I'd cut back on my time at work, handing more of the reins over to Paul so I could spend more time with Oliver, particularly when he traveled for shows.

He'd found it difficult to stay at his apartment alone after Ben had broken in and I needed to feel him near, to be able to reach out and touch him throughout the night and remind myself that he was safe. We quickly agreed to let our individual leases go and bought a house together. It was cozy and peaceful and sat along a private stretch of beach. It was perfect for the two of us, allowing us to shut out the rest of the world and simply focus on each other and it had gone a long way in helping with the healing process.

Brooklyn was in her sophomore year at college but came home as often as she could to see us. She and Oliver had become extreme-ly close after his attack and they continue to talk on the phone al-most every day. Gayle was just as close to him and was currently teaching Oliver to cook. Andrew and I enjoyed the fruits of their labor, but preferred to hang out in the living room, watching basket-ball together instead.

Oliver and I were happier than we'd ever been and that's why we'd chosen this day, exactly one year after his attack, to get mar-ried. We'd been through hell and back over the last year, but we'd triumphed through it all and come out even stronger as a couple. It was important to both of us that we wipe away the last of the evil that Ben had left behind and start the next year full of love and hope and promises to each other.

We had a private ceremony right on the beach with just our closest friends and family. I could hear Brooklyn and Gayle sniffling as I'd recited my vows and Oliver's eyes had sparkled in the sunlight as he gazed up at me. There was so much love in those eyes, more than I ever thought I'd have in my life and I knew what it truly meant to be rich.

"We need to get going soon or we'll miss our flight," I whispered several hours later as I held him close. Our guests had all left and we were enjoying a few quiet moments out on the back deck before we had to leave for our honeymoon.

Oliver burrowed his face in my neck as we swayed to the music and I shivered when I felt his lips press against my skin. "Just one more song," he said dreamily.

I smiled and pulled him closer, breathing in his sweet scent as we danced in the moonlight with the sound of waves crashing nearby. I'd never known a more perfect moment and it was all because of the man in my arms, my husband. After another song had come and gone, I used a finger to lift his chin and kissed him softly.

"We really do need to go," I reminded him.

"Fine," he said with a long, playful sigh. I smacked him on the ass and he let out a small yelp.

"Easy with the goods there, sir," he joked, rubbing a hand over the abused area.

I bent down and spoke into his ear. "If you don't go inside and get your bags, then I'll really have to put you over my knee."

Oliver's eyes grew darker and he let out that little whimper I loved so much. "And what if that's what I want you to do?" he breathed.

A low growl tore from my chest and Oliver tossed a wink at

me before sauntering off to gather his things, his hips swaying sexily from side to side. My smile grew until I felt sure it would split my face wide open. I headed into the house after him and raced up the steps to make sure he'd remembered to pack my favorite high heels of his. There was no doubt in my mind that life with Oliver was going to be one adventure after another, and I couldn't wait for it to begin.

The End

ACKNOWLEDGEMENTS

As always, my first thanks go to my family; my husband, my children, my siblings and my parents. You have stood by my side from the moment I said I wanted to write my first book. You offered your support, your wisdom and your encouragement and none of this would have become a reality without you. I love you guys. You are my heart and soul.

Thank you to Deena for always standing by my side. No matter what I do, you are always there, supporting me and loving me and that is such a unique and priceless thing to find. Your friendship gives me the strength to try new things, while knowing that I will never be doing it alone. I love you.

Thank you to Jenn. When I first dreamed up this story, you were the very first person I wanted to tell. I just knew I needed to hear your thoughts on it. Was it too different? Was it too out there? Could I even make it work? You responded immediately with, "This is the book I've been waiting for." Throughout this entire process, you've been right there, encouraging me, pushing me and talking me through it. You believed in me when I had trouble believing in myself and for that, I will always be grateful. You are my best friend, my sister, my person. I will ALWAYS choose you!

Thank you to my team: My editor, Allison Holzapfel, Jay Aheer of Simply Defined Art, Judy Zweifler of Judy's Proofreading, Stacey

Blake of Champagne Formats and my betas; Jenn Gibson, Lee Rey, Meredith King, Lori Greis, Morningstar Ashley, Luna David, Anita Ford, Andy Rogers, Kerry S., Michael Bailey and Jaclyn Quinn. You have shown me more support, encouragement and enthusiasm than I could ever repay you for. Thank you all from the bottom of my heart.

ABOUT THE AUTHOR

I am married to my high school sweetheart who let's face it, is a saint for putting up with me all of these years. Together we have been blessed with the chance to raise two amazing human beings and so far, we haven't screwed it up; I'll let you know for sure later. I love watching movies, cooking, going to the beach and spending time with my family and best friends. I am an obsessive reader who is a complete sucker for a good love story but loves to feel a broad range of emotions throughout a book. I think real life is hard enough and so my books offer twists and turns, but always with a happy ending.

I love to hear from my readers. You can reach me at:

Twitter
twitter.com/annabellamicha1

Facebook
www.facebook.com/profile.php?id=100011438515157

Annabella's Sexy Souls
www.facebook.com/groups/233274880449097/

Blog
annabellamichaels.blogspot.com

AUTHOR RECOMMENDED BOOKS

LUNA DAVID

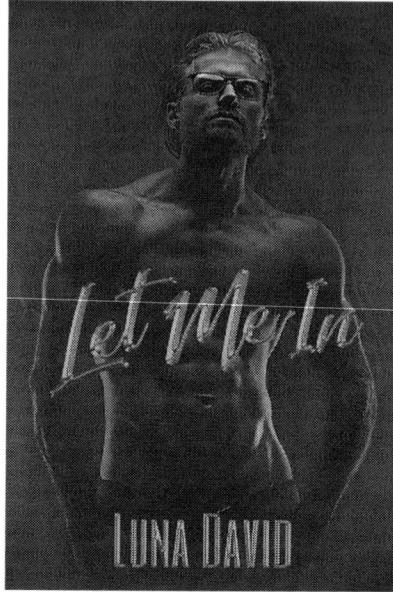

Twenty-year-old Liam Cavanagh works three dead-end-jobs to take care of his family. He's been the sole breadwinner since he was fifteen and yearns for a life of his own. Forced to grow up too fast, he carries the burdens of responsibilities that shouldn't be his, and it's slowly destroying him. The more he tries to control, the more out of control he feels.

When he gets a hit on a personal ad he placed on The Boys Club app, he shrugs it off as impossible. With nearly 600 miles between him and Daddy Cash he thought the odds were stacked against them until Cash's current boy convinces him otherwise and persuades Liam to take on the role of Daddy's new boy.

Saying forty-year-old entrepreneur Cash Moreau is having a bad week is an understatement. The man he's been with for years leaves him for a new job, his own company is in crisis, and to top it all off, a young stranger shows up on his doorstep with all his worldly possessions, claiming to be his new boy. Liam wants a Daddy to depend on, and Cash refuses to believe he's what's best for Liam.

Despite their powerful connection, Cash finally pushes Liam away, and the beautiful boy who stole his heart disappears. Soon, Cash realizes what he's let slip through his fingers. The elusive thing he's been searching for is Liam, it's only ever been Liam, and suddenly Cash will move heaven and earth to find what he's lost. Will he find his boy in time to make things right, or is it too late to let him in?

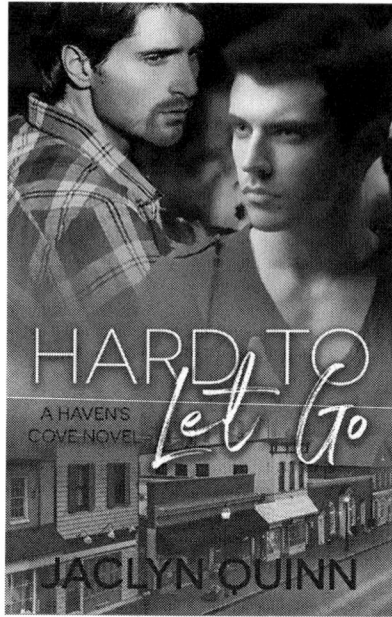

Owen Richards lives a quiet life in his small hometown of Haven's Cove. He has a rewarding life consisting of three very supportive—not to mention feisty—women, and a successful bakery that he owns and absolutely loves. Yet, Owen can't seem to shake this emptiness inside or the intense feeling that something is missing. A sudden encounter with a man from his past, one he despises, turns his entire world upside down. When Owen finds himself attracted to that sexy man, he questions everything, including his sanity. After all, only an incredibly disturbed person would find that he can't stop thinking about his high school bully.

Brody Walker never expected to return to Haven's Cove. He's made a life for himself in Boston, where he can truly be the person he was always meant to be. But an unexpected call has Brody facing all the demons he'd left behind so long ago. Now, he's faced with not only a difficult goodbye, but one long overdue apology to a man who is no longer that lanky kid from high school. The challenge is to convince the guy he's changed—and also prove he's worth taking a chance on.

When passions ignite truths are exposed, changing the beliefs these men have held on to for years. Faced with the knowledge that things aren't always what they seem, will they choose to hold on to the incredible thing they've found...or is it easier to give in to the fear and let go?

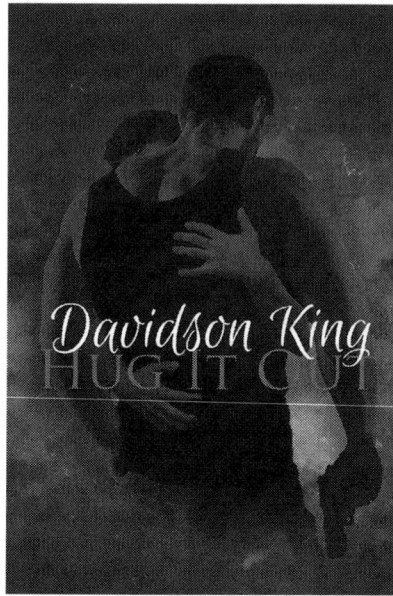

Riordan Darcy has spent the last fourteen years building a name for himself as a notorious assassin. He travels the world taking the lives of some of the worst humanity has to offer, leaving his signature on every victim.

Riordan becomes unhappy and withdrawn from the world after a job goes horribly wrong and he makes the decision to get out of the life he was forced into, so long ago. When his meddling, older sister gives him a birthday gift that's impossible to refuse, his plans to leave his life of crime take a backseat when he's forced to protect the life of a veritable stranger.

When professional hugger and TLC provider, Teddy Harris, is offered a month-long companionship contract, he's hard pressed to turn it down. Cuddler by day and a video game reviewer by night, Teddy's need to make people feel loved and cared for is what drives him. When he meets Riordan Darcy, professional challenge and personal temptation collide, making it nearly impossible for him to endure a whole month with the gorgeous, enigmatic man without falling head over heels in love.

When a mole is discovered within Riordan's organization, relationships are compromised, and people's lives are in danger. Time isn't on their side, and they discover answers can't always be found by hugging it out when someone is hell-bent on eliminating each and every one of them. Can Riordan and Teddy survive long enough to fall in love, or will they die trying?

25782535R00117

Made in the USA
Columbia, SC
07 September 2018